Chel

MW00882399

By: Sean Hunter

A Molding Messengers Publication

Chelby's Hairoics

Copyright © 2022 by Sean Hunter

All rights reserved. Printed in the United States of America. No part of this book may be used or reproduced in any manner whatsoever without written permission except in the case of brief quotations embodied in critical articles or reviews.

This book is a work of fiction. Names, characters, businesses, organizations, places, events and incidents either are the product of the author's imagination or are used fictitiously. Any resemblance to actual persons, living or dead, events, or locales is entirely coincidental.

For information about permission to reproduce selections from this book, Write to Molding Messengers, LLC at 1728 NE Miami Gardens Drive, Suite #111, North Miami Beach, FL, 33179 or email Info.Staff@MoldingMessengers.com or visit www.MoldingMessengers.com

Library of Congress Control Number: 2021924501

Print ISBN: 978-0-578-33636-7

eBook ISBN: 978-0-578-33637-4

A Molding Messengers Publication

Acknowledgment

Writing a book is more complex than I thought but more rewarding than I could have ever imagined. None of this could have been possible without God, the Creator of all. He has blessed me with the ability to inspire people to be better through my writing. I only pray that HE continues to allow me to reach people with my words and through HIS grace.

I'm eternally grateful to my father Marcus; may he rest in peace. Ten years ago, the same year he passed, he told me that he loved my writing and that I should look into making it a career. Among all the tools, morals, and values my father has left me with to groom me into becoming a good man, this was just another insightful gem he has given me to prove he mainly was always right. Well, Dad, I finally listened, and I'm going to make it happen.

To my wife Akia and children Cheyenne, Lauren, and Sean. Thank you for being you. Thank you for the inspiration to finish what I said I would. Everything I do is for all of you. Thank you for allowing me to read draft pages of the book week after week to each of you and giving me the necessary feedback to push forward. Whether I was exhausted after a 12-hour shift, or frustrated with the outside world, just looking at your faces when I came home gave me the push to continue writing.

To the rest of my family, my loving mother, Vilma: has been supportive since I was a child, always backing me in whatever I do or say I could do. Thank you for always being there. To my younger but not little brother Brian, I'm pretty sure he thought to himself, a book? He supported; either way, I'm so thankful for that. To my sister Tashe, thank you for believing in me.

To my always supportive and insightful uncle Claude who I call Junior, thank you for always being there through all the ups and downs. To my aunts, Penny and Valerie, thank you for always being there and giving me feedback on some of my writing. To my uncle and aunt Reggie and Martha, thank you for the support. To my father and mother-in-law, Richard and Regina Harris, I appreciate your feedback and advice to continue my writing. To my brother and sister-in-law Kevyn and Karyn, I thank you for all the support. To my uncle, Michael, I thank you for your kind words and forever support. To my Aunt Robin, thank you for all the feedback and support.

To my friends: Josephine Andres, Chadsity Hernandez, Sharlene Farquharson, Kandice Lunnon, Ann Harkless, Leonie S. Peters, Kenya Vaughn, Lisa D. Brewster, and Tiffany De Roche, who have supported me from day one through this entire process, thank you. I appreciate you taking the time to read and then give all thoughts, feedback, and critiques, making me a better writer.

To the Molding Messengers staff, I appreciate and thank you for your professionalism and patience throughout this process. I thank you for always being accessible via emails and or phone calls. I thank you for being author-friendly and motivated by putting forth a great product over everything else. It meant a lot to a first-time author.

I especially must thank my editor, Ms. Vanessa Russell, for doing an outstanding job. She was a pleasure to work with, and I hope to work with her on future projects. Being extremely professional and thorough,

Vanessa was a big part of helping me put forth the best quality book.

Finally, I have to acknowledge who helped bring the idea of this book from thought to paper. My oldest daughter Cheyenne, who at nine years old is already an avid reader and writer, inspired me to finish what we started with hopes of not disappointing her. I hope I made you proud, baby. Through the grace of God, I know I will.

Chelby's Hairoics

By: Sean Hunter

A Molding Messengers Publication

Introduction

"It hurts, Mom! It hurts!" Chelby whispered as the EMTs rushed her into the back of the ambulance.

Her mother was visibly shaken up by what she just witnessed as tears flowed down her face. "I'm right here, baby. I'm right here," her mother murmured as she ran alongside the EMTs.

The rain began to pour as firefighters rushed to the scene. A small crowd began to gather around as the salon went up in flames. Mia did not even notice as she got up onto the ambulance, with Chelby's current state surrounding her focus. Mia sat close to her only child, praying in a light whisper that she would make it through.

The EMTs worked on Chelby's vital signs as the ambulance raced through traffic to get to the hospital. Not the sounds of the sirens, beeping horns of the traffic, nor the thunder from above could impede Mia's concerns.

As the ambulance arrived at the hospital, Chelby slightly looked up at her mother to ask, "Will I be ok, Mom?"

Her mother's heart skipped a beat with water building in her eyes, but she replied, "Yes, baby. God will protect you."

Chapter 1

Meeting Chelby

Over the summer, a few months prior, Chelby and her parents Amia and Marcus Williams moved into a new three-bedroom apartment in Queens, NY. Chelby was both nervous and excited about moving to a new school and neighborhood. She was popular at her old school for being both smart and helpful, but this was a new school, and she knew she would have to adjust to her new environment.

This year, Chelby would be entering the sixth grade, and change can be challenging for any 11-year-old. Her mother, Amia, was a hairdresser for seven years. She was finally able to buy and own her first salon, an accomplishment that any young budding entrepreneur would marvel at, in which Amia took great pride. Chelby loved to frequent the salon her mother use to work at so she could observe how the other professionals styled hair. Unfortunately, because it was so far away, she couldn't visit as often as she would've like. Her mother's new salon was close to their new apartment and Chelby's new school though, so she could stop by as often as she'd like.

Chelby enjoyed anytime with her mother, especially when asked to help around the shop, and since Amia's clients thought the world of Chelby, they would allow her to help Amia wash their hair from time to time. Both the old salon and old school were in a rougher, less safe part of Queens, known as the Southside. Chelby witnessed her mother work long hours on the weekends, and that generally was the only time the two would travel together.

Amia, who went by Mia for short, was a sweet and kind person. She loved to talk, which helped grow friendships amongst her customers. She was a baby face full-figured woman with a caramel complexion and long

3

jet-black hair that reached a little above the middle of her back. Amia was 32 years old and a little above the average height for a woman. She was educated and practiced using common sense.

Most who came to know Amia would agree that she was candidly sharp. Although Amia had beautiful long hair, she didn't show it off most days. Since Amia was always on the go, it was usually out in its natural state, or a simple ponytail would do just fine for her. Juggling between being a wife, mother, and new entrepreneur was not always easy, yet she managed it all with love and dedication, which spoke volumes of the well-rounded woman she was.

Chelby's father, Marcus, worked for a trucking company, so he was on the road a lot. Marcus was a tall, stocky, dark complexion man with a silly side that didn't match his stern-looking exterior. Although he chose not to finish school to make money at his current full-time job, he is street-smart and knowledgeable; it wouldn't be easy to pull a fast one on him, indeed.

Marcus was 35 years old, but from seeing him in person, he didn't look a year over thirty, especially if you'd asked him. Marcus would go back and forth between a full beard and a goatee, but either seemed to suit him well. He is both a great husband and father, strong-willed but kind and thoughtful as well. Marcus always made sure to make it to all of Chelby's school events and award ceremonies. Although he worked in Long Island during the week, when Chelby would ask her father to make any event, his response would always be, "Somehow, someway, I'll be there!"

Chelby's mother was tough on her when it came to education. She deemed it necessary to go far and beyond giving average effort and would not accept anything less. Both of her parents taught her the importance of being disciplined and practicing good habits. Balancing principles, values, and leisure time are what her parents were great at and instilled these morals in her early.

They were a close-knit family, always out together on the weekends, whether it be restaurants, movies, or bowling, they could be seen routinely together as a loving family. The bond between the three is what Chelby cherished the most.

* * *

The first day of school seemed to come so fast, according to Chelby. Usually, on the Sunday before school, Chelby would think of three outfits to wear and ultimately pick her favorite one out of the three. Naturally indecisive, she would end up making a final choice at the last minute. This time, however, Chelby remembered that her new school required students to wear uniforms. Although that saved some time, it was getting late, and Amia still hadn't done Chelby's hair for the week coming up.

Generally, on Sundays Amia would give her a different hairstyle, depending on what she requested for that week. Chelby enjoyed getting her hair done and loved the fact that her mother could do any of the different latest hairstyles for her.

"Ok, baby, while the food is in the oven, let me start doing your hair," Mia said, calling down the hallway.

"Yes, coming, Mom!" Chelby answered from her room.

Chelby hurried to her parent's room to get what was needed. With a comb, hair grease, and flat iron in hand, she yelled a question down the hallway at her mother.

"Hey, Mom. Where's the tiny rubber bands at?"

"The same place you left them, on top of the dresser, and bring the brush as well!" Her mother responded.

Chelby hustled with all the things her mom needed to the living room and laid everything out for her on the couch. As she sat in between her mother's legs with her mother on the couch above her, she tried to narrow down what she wanted to have done in her mind.

"Ok, baby, so how would you like your hair done for your first day of school?" Mia asked.

"Mom, I can't decide. Can you just pick a style this time for me, please?" Chelby excitedly responded.

"Ok, baby, I got you," her mother replied. As her mother began to style her hair, Chelby winced and moaned. She fought through the pain without any complaints only because she knew that it'd all be worth the temporary discomfort.

Halfway into the process, Amia's phone started to ring, so she stopped doing Chelby's hair to answer her cell phone. It was her father calling to speak to Chelby before she went to bed. On this particular day, Marcus was running a little late in traffic, driving from Long Island to Queens.

"Hello," Mia answered.

"What's up babe? How are you?" Marcus asked.

"I'm good, and yourself?" Before he could answer, she blurted out, "But listen, I'm rushing trying to finish up your daughter's hair and still have dinner cooking in the oven, so you have to be quick," Mia responded hastily.

"Ok, cool, FaceTime me so I can speak to Chelby real quick, please," Marcus requested.

Marcus abruptly got off the highway onto the service road and pulled over to await Mia's call back. Mia hung up and FaceTimed Marcus, so he'd be able to see and speak to Chelby before she went to bed. Chelby got excited as she FaceTimed her father. Marcus hated getting home too late to kiss Chelby goodnight before she went to sleep.

"Hey baby, how are you? Ready for school tomorrow?" Her father asked.

"Hey Dad, I'm good, but I'm kind of nervous and excited about tomorrow," Chelby responded as she smiled anxiously.

"I know you may be a little nervous, but don't be. You make friends everywhere you go, and you know that. As long as you be yourself and do the right thing as you always do, you'll be just fine," Marcus encouraged.

"Thanks, Dad. Have a goodnight!" Chelby replied.

"Love you, baby, and have a goodnight as well," Marcus said as he ended the call. After ending the call, Marcus got back onto the highway and continued home.

Back home, Chelby didn't even notice that her mother was finished with her hair because she was so enthused over conversing with her father before going to bed. "Mom, you finished already?!" Chelby questioned.

"That's right, so go take a look real quick and come back, plus you still have to eat. It's getting late," Mia responded.

Chelby ran back into her mother's room to look into the big mirror, which was part of the door outside her parents' bedroom. She picked up a small, handheld mirror from the dresser to see both the front and back of her hair. As she did this, she thought to herself about how great of a hairdresser her mother was.

From above, she could see that her hair had a part going from the middle of her head, leading towards the back of her head. On both sides of the parted hair were two thick braids starting from the front of her head, rounding off inches above each ear but curving and ending a little above each shoulder. From either side of

9

her head, Chelby saw three small parts, with two tiny braids in between each, about half an inch apart from each small braid. Chelby noticed that on the sides were tiny braids connecting into the other long thick braids evenly, completing Chelby's new hairstyle for her first day of school.

"Twin braids?!" she whispered as she slowly did a 360-turn using both mirrors. Chelby knew most of all the braided hairstyles' names and took pride in her knowledge of such. She yelled down the hall into the kitchen where her mother was preparing dinner. "It looks beautiful, Mom. I love it. Thank you so much!"

"You're very welcome, baby, but come sit down and eat dinner. It's starting to get late, "her mother exclaimed.

School started in the middle of the week this year, which also meant that tonight was Taco Tuesday. Chelby loved her mother's cooking, just as much as she loved how she did hair, so she looked forward to Taco Tuesdays. As she walked towards the kitchen table, her eyes lit up with joy.

"Yessss, Taco Tuesday!" Chelby screamed out. *So, I guess that's what was in the oven,* she thought to herself.

"Yes, but don't forget to pray before you eat, Chelby," her mother demanded. So Chelby did just that.

"God is good. God is great. Thank you, God, for our food. In Jesus' name, AMEN!" Chelby recited. Her mother echoed an 'Amen' from the kitchen as well. After eating, Chelby cleaned the table then headed to the bathroom to brush her teeth and take a quick shower.

Once she finished in the bathroom, Chelby dried off, put on lotion and her PJs, then headed to bed. She read mostly every night before going to sleep, mainly to help her sleep well. She enjoyed reading a lot; it was one of her top favorite things to do. Usually, any fantasy book would do just fine. Tonight, she was reading an old Rainbow Magic book, which did just the trick.

Ten minutes after she fell asleep, her father's key unlocked the door. As he walked in, he gave Amia a quick hug and kiss before walking swiftly to Chelby's room.

Marcus's boots echoed down the hallway as he approached. His smile and wishful thinking soon turned into a frown with empty hopes once arriving at her doorway.

Disappointed, he arched over to kiss Chelby on the forehead as she laid in her bed dreaming. "Look at my big girl," Marcus whispered, looking over Chelby. Closing his eyes as he stood over her, he whispered a short prayer that she slept well before exiting her room.

The following day Chelby woke up anxious but excited about school. The unknown always made Chelby uneasy, but over the years, she had gotten better with her anxiety. She ate the breakfast her mother had laid out for her, buttered toast with turkey bacon, then went into the bathroom to wash up and brush her teeth. She put on her uniform, which she noticed, had at least one of her two favorite colors. The new school uniform was blue and gold, and her favorite colors were purple and blue.

The one thing that helped her confidence and made her less anxious was when she unwrapped her headscarf, checking out how her new hairstyle looked in the mirror.

Wow, Mom did a great job, she thought to herself. She put her shoes on and grabbed her bag to head out as her mother waited for her in the car. As she walked outside, her mother yelled out the car window, "Make sure you have everything Chelby, but please hurry up! I still have to head to the bank after I drop you off at school, then go open up the new shop."

Chelby listened and picked up the pace to get to the car. Her mother pulled off in a rush as soon as she knew Chelby was in and secured. "Chelby, you have your seatbelt on, right?" Mia asked.

"Yes, I do, Mom," Chelby replied.

As they raced to the school, the radio wasn't up too high but loud enough for Chelby to sing and dance along in her seat. Whatever dance moves you could make in a chair that you were seat belted to, she made them like a star.

Once arriving at school, Chelby kissed her mother on the cheek and hugged her goodbye before leaving the car. "Have a great day today, baby, and come by the shop straight after school. Love you!" Her mother said as she waved goodbye and zoomed off.

As Chelby walked into the front entrance, she looked and listened for directions to the gymnasium. For the first day, all school classes would be meeting there first thing in the morning so that all students, along with their new teachers, would be together and proceed to their designated classrooms shortly after that.

Chelby already knew this from the information her mother gathered after attending a school meeting the week before school began. At the meeting, her mother learned her teacher's name and classroom number as well: Ms. Spiegal, class 6-201. There was a teacher at the very next set of doors from the entrance, directing both students and parents towards the gym.

As Chelby got closer to the gym, she began to get more and more nervous. She took in a deep breath, and after a slow exhale, she continued. Entering the gym, she surveyed the gym briefly, both looking for her class number and seeing if she noticed any familiar faces. A sprinkle here and there, Chelby knew from other extracurricular activities she was into outside of school, such as the tennis club she joined over the summer. A few others she knew from the neighborhood, but nowhere near the number of friends she had at her old school.

Once reaching where her class was standing up, she figured that she must have been earlier than she originally had thought. Only a few classmates were in line with her. She counted seven boys and one other girl. So Chelby just stood there and waited for further instructions.

"Hey, I love your hair, girl!" the girl in her class said.

Chelby looked around briefly to make sure that the girl was speaking to her and then quickly murmured, "Who mine? Thank you!"

The girl was short and pretty, with a light skin complexion and a warm smile. She looked too young to be in the sixth grade, but as Chelby learned from experience, looks were deceiving. Chelby, of course, noticed her long beautiful hair as well.

"You're welcome. I love that style. It must have taken you all day to get done," the girl replied.

"It was actually done pretty fast. My mother did it," Chelby admitted.

"Wow, your mother has skills! By the way, I'm Shyla," the girl mentioned.

"Oh, I'm Chelby, and my mother owns a hair salon, so she does my hair all the time," Chelby responded.

"Wow, that's cool. Maybe I can come by sometime. What's the name of it?" Shyla asked.

"It's called Mia's Marvelous Hair Salon. It's not too far from the school," Chelby exclaimed.

Shyla's face was suddenly overcome with excitement. "Wait, that new spot that just opened up over the summer, a few blocks down, that's your mother's salon?" Shyla asked, excitedly. "Oh yeah, I gotta tell my mother this, I'm gonna be in there every week, so get used to me!" Shyla exclaimed.

"Yup, that's the one. I'm going by there straight after school if you want to come with me," Chelby replied.

"Oh, ok, cool, I usually have dance three times a week, but that doesn't start until next week. So, I'm there!" Shyla responded.

As they continued to talk, more and more students began to file in by the bunches. They rushed in, some with and some without their parents. Shyla told Chelby that she's been going to that school since the first grade and that the school was excellent. Shyla added that the teachers genuinely wanted the best for their students, even if, at times, they were annoying. The voices in the gym seemed to get louder and louder as the crowd of people grew.

Shyla then mentioned that the students there were diverse, as Chelby briefly checked her surroundings. The different faces in the gym, both young and old, proved this to be true and different from Chelby's old school, which had predominately African American students. Chelby didn't mind at all. Not only was it in her personality to love all, but she was also taught not to see color by her parents. Judging people on their merits and actions and not on how they look are some of the principles she believed and stood for.

A few students would walk over to Shyla to say hi, and Shyla would immediately introduce them to Chelby. Chelby thought this was so cool of Shyla and was glad Shyla didn't mind doing this. It made things more comfortable for Chelby.

Once all the students were in the gymnasium with their assigned classes, the teachers did a quick roll call before heading upstairs. Amongst all the noise and confusion, Chelby noticed one teacher, he seemed to be fussing with two of his students angrily. The teacher was pointing and waving his finger at them, even grabbing one by the wrist and forcing that student to the back of the line.

He was a tall and slender man with black and grey hair on his head and in his goatee, sharply dressed in a brown three-piece suit; this particular teacher seemed overdressed amongst his colleagues. His voice was deep but not overly loud when speaking to the young students, and he had a stern look to go along with his aggressive tone.

"What's the deal with that guy, Shyla?" Chelby asked.

"Who, Mr. McIntosh? Yeah, he's not on my favorite teacher's list. I really don't mess with that guy at all. He's always given me bad vibes!" Shyla stated. "I don't think he's too fond of our kind, either," Shyla continued.

Chelby paused a second before responding to Shyla. "Our kind, you mean, girls, females?"

Shyla got closer to Chelby. "Nah, I mean, our kind," Shyla said, pointing to the skin on her hand.

Chelby initially looked confused, which abruptly shifted to anger written throughout her face. "He's racist?" Chelby blurted out. Shyla put one finger over Chelby's mouth.

"He teaches 2nd grade, I think it's class 203, and from what I know, most of his students either don't like him or are afraid of him," Shyla said. "Some of the older kids even call him C-Mac, and the C stands for cruel!" Shyla murmured. "He's only been teaching here for a couple of years, though, so he's kinda new. But I heard he's cool with the superintendent, so I guess he's been teaching for like forever. Maybe it's hard to get him out. I don't know," Shyla explained.

"That's insane. Nobody should be treated like that, especially little kids!" Chelby replied.

Ms. Spiegal started walking the class out of the gym but as Chelby followed her class upstairs she couldn't get Mr. McIntosh's behavior out of her head. One thing Chelby was very passionate about was being righteous. She hated to see people of any age mistreated, but it hit a sore spot when it happened to kids.

Something has to be done about that man, she thought to herself as she continued with her day.

* * *

Chelby's first day of school at a new school went better than expected. She loved her new teacher, Ms. Spiegal, and she thought that the students at the new school were pleasantly friendly and kind as well.

During classroom announcements, Ms. Spiegal mentioned to the class that starting the following Monday, the school would introduce a new program for 6th graders. It was a volunteer program in which the chosen volunteers would tutor and mentor students in grades ranging from 1st to 3rd. It would be twice a week and taken place in the school's main library directly after school for an hour each time.

That immediately interested Chelby. She enjoyed helping and giving back every chance she could. She couldn't wait to sign up and did so as soon as the opportunity came up after school. Once she was done signing up, she headed downstairs to meet up with Shyla who was in front, waiting for Chelby as she had hoped.

"What's up Shyla, you ready?" Chelby asked.

"Of course, what took you so long?" Shyla replied.

"Oh, my fault, I went to sign up for that volunteering thing starting next week. How come you didn't sign up?" Chelby asked.

"Oh nahhhhhhhhhh, I'll pass. I have a little brother. That's all the volunteer work I can handle," Shyla responded. They both giggled and proceeded to head to Chelby's mother's shop.

On the way there, Shyla told Chelby about how long she's been dancing for and her aspirations to pursue it as she got older. Shyla also mentioned her love for singing, rapping, and gymnastics as they walked to the salon.

"Hey Chelby, when's your birthday? What's your sign?" Shyla asked.

"Oh, it's February 5th, and I'm an Aquarius. What's yours?" Chelby responded.

"Aquarius, huh, that's cool, so you must be really creative then? Mine is July 14th, a Cancer," Shyla replied.

"Oh nice, a summer birthday, but why would you say I must be creative?" Chelby asked.

Shyla smirked before responding. "I kinda find astrology interesting, so I know a little about it, and one of your sign characteristics is being creative. Is it true?"

"Wow, that's cool. Well, I did use to write a lot when I was younger, even won some contests at my old school, but I don't write as much as I use to," Chelby admitted.

"So, see, you are creative," Shyla replied.

"Yeah, I guess you're right. So, what are some of the traits of a Cancer sign?" Chelby asked.

"So glad that you asked, boo, cause we are the best!" Shyla shouted and laughed. "No, but seriously, we are kind but tough, and most importantly, extremely loyal to our friends and loved ones. So obviously, you can't go wrong with me," Shyla said with a smile.

This girl was so confident in herself, Chelby thought.

Once finally arriving at the salon, as they entered, Chelby was proud to show off her mother's new shop. It was bigger than the one her mother worked out of in Southside Jamaica, Queens. More important than the shop's size for Chelby was the fact that her mother owned it.

"So, this is it, Shyla, what you think?" Chelby asked.

"Yooooooo, this spot is lit! I'll be back here this weekend for sure!" Shyla replied.

Chelby smiled as she walked Shyla to where her mother was. She waved and said hi to all the hairdressers before reaching her mother, as they smiled and waved back to her as well. As they approached Mia, Chelby purposely bumped Shyla to whisper her mother's name to her, just in case she forgot.

"Hey, Mom. How are you doing?" Chelby asked.

"Hey, boo, how are you? How was school? Tell me everything. By the way, who is your friend?" Mia asked.

"Oh, and this is Shyla, she's in my class, and school was great! Everybody was really nice and friendly, and I like my teacher so far too. By the way, Mom, I signed up for this volunteer program starting next week, for two days a week, for an hour right after school," Chelby answered.

"Slow down, Chelby. You're all excitable!" Mia looked over at Shyla. "Nice to meet you, Shyla. You're such a pretty young lady. I'm Mrs. Williams, but you can call me Mrs. Mia, ok?" Mia said as she greeted Shyla. Mia then turned her attention back to Chelby. "That's awesome, Chelby. I'm so glad you had a great first day. You have to explain to me more about that volunteer program, though," Mia responded.

"Thank you so much, Mrs. Mia, and your shop is beautiful! I'm going to tell my mother about it soon as I get home," Shyla replied. "Thank you, sweetie, and please do. You and your mother are welcomed anytime," Mia responded.

"Hey Chelby, do me a favor and get me some more conditioner from the bottom drawer, please," Mia asked. "No problem, Mom, here you go," Chelby said after handing her mother what she needed. "So back to what I was saying, Mom, we would be helping mentor and tutor younger kids in our school from 1st to 3rd grade. It sounds really cool to me," Chelby exclaimed.

"That does sound good Chelby, just make sure that it doesn't affect your grades, baby, and it's fine with me," Mia responded.

"Ok, Mom. It won't," Chelby replied.

It was starting to get a little late, and Shyla still had to travel home. Shyla tugged at Chelby's hood to get her attention. "Hey, Chelby, I'm about to leave out. I still have to take a bus home, and it hardly comes the later it gets," Shyla admitted.

"Oh, ok. Thank you so much for coming with me. I appreciate you introducing me to your friends this morning, too," Chelby responded.

"Oh, that was nada. I'll see you tomorrow," Shyla replied. "Thanks for letting me come through Mrs. Mia. I really love your salon!" Shyla admitted.

"Thank you so much, sweetie. Take this card for you and your mother. It has the number and hours of the shop in the front and back. I hope to see you this weekend. Get home safely, dear," Mia replied.

"Thank you, Mrs. Mia, have a goodnight, everybody," Shyla shouted, leaving the shop.

"She seems nice, Chelby. I'm glad you made a new friend today," Chelby's mother said. "Yeah, she's really cool, Mom," Chelby replied.

"So, listen, baby, let me finish up with my customer cause I know it's going to start to get busy in the next hour or so. So go sit down, and if I or any of the other ladies need you, we'll call you, ok?" Chelby's mother instructed.

"Ok, Mom, just let me know," Chelby replied.

Chelby read a few magazines placed on the table next to the couch to let the time pass. Every now and again, she would get up to see the different hairstyles some customers received that day. Her mother was finally finished with her last customer and was ready to go home for the night.

Before they left, Mia gave instructions to a woman on her staff scheduled to close up the salon. After wishing the rest of the ladies a good night, she got her things together to leave. The remaining ladies in the shop waved to Chelby goodnight as Mia and Chelby exited the salon. Chelby was starving as usual at this time, and in fact, so was her mother.

"So, what are you gonna make for dinner tonight, Mom?" Chelby asked.

"I have a taste for some pasta, so something along those lines," Mia responded.

"Do we have garlic bread?" Chelby asked.

"Yes, baby, I think I do," Mia replied.

"Ok, good," Chelby answered. They both got into the car and drove home.

Later that weekend, Chelby's new friend Shyla returned to the salon, bringing her mother along with her this time. Shyla and her mother got a wash and set, as all four ladies got to know one another better through great conversation.

* * *

The following week during Phys-ed, Shyla wouldn't stop talking about how good a hairdresser Chelby's mother was to Shyla's other friends. She mentioned how good the salon looked inside and how great a job Ms. Mia did with her mother's hair. That made Chelby so proud, but she humbly smiled and nodded her head when asked about the shop.

This week was the start of the volunteer program. Chelby was chosen to be a volunteer and was super excited about it. After school, she went straight to the main library as Shyla went to dance. Chelby saw her name posted up on the board attached to the wall, and next to it was the name of the student she was assigned to tutor.

Cameron Michaels from class 2-203, Mr. McIntosh's class. Cameron was already in the library, waiting in a chair with his bookbag directly next to him in another. He was looking down at the table in front of him as he doodled on a piece of paper. Cameron was a short handsome second grader. He had a short haircut and seemed shy from the lack of eye contact he made with Chelby. His brown skin complexion matched with his light hazel eyes made Chelby think he was so cute.

"Hi Cameron, how are you? I'm Chelby, your tutor," Chelby said.

"Hi Chelby, I was waiting for you," Cameron replied.

"So, Cameron, I thought I'd go over your homework with you, and afterward, you can choose a book we can read together, cool?" Chelby asked.

"Yes, Chelby, that's cool," Cameron responded.

So, after finishing up on Cameron's homework, Cameron decided to pick out a goosebump book to read. As they were about to read the book, Chelby stopped to ask Cameron a question.

"Hey Cameron, how does Mr. McIntosh treat you in class?" Chelby questioned.

Cameron's facial expressions went from happy to sad within seconds. He just shook his head, but Chelby could tell something was wrong from his response. "Does he yell at you, hit you, or mistreat you, Cameron?" Chelby asked.

"Umm, I don't want to talk about it," Cameron whispered.

"If there's something he's doing to you or anyone else you know about, you have to say something. If you don't, it will continue and get worse," Chelby explained. "Please, Chelby, I don't want to talk about it," Cameron murmured. "Can we please just finish reading?" Cameron begged in a light whisper.

"Uh-huh, we'll talk about this another time Cameron, please continue reading," Chelby responded.

Later that night, Chelby continued to replay Cameron's facial reaction over and over in her mind. She could barely even eat dinner, which was extremely rare for her. She would take a bite or two and then look out into space before taking another few bites. She felt compelled to get to the bottom of what was going on with that teacher.

Her mother noticed Chelby's slow eating after glancing at her from the kitchen. "Hey baby, are you ok? You don't like the food?" Mia asked.

"Huh? Oh nah, I was just thinking about something," Chelby explained.

"I know that look, baby. Something is bothering you. What's on your mind?" Her mother curiously asked.

"I don't know, Mom, this teacher at school. I'm not feeling him at all," Chelby answered.

"This teacher you're talking about, did he disrespect you in some way?" Chelby's mother asked.

"No, but I've witnessed him being mean to his students on the first day of school, and now I think he may have mistreated the little boy I tutor as well," Chelby replied.

"Wow, did that little boy tell you that?" Mia asked.

"No, not exactly, Mom, but his body language and facial expressions changed once I asked about the teacher to him," Chelby responded.

"Well, you can't just assume, Chelby. You may have to look further into it since it seems to be bothering you so much," Mia replied.

"You're right, Mom, and I will, but you know I'm usually right when I've gotten feelings like this before about certain things," Chelby replied.

"That's true, Chelby, but I hope this time your gut feeling is wrong," Mia responded. Chelby finished her dinner that night and went to bed with the dilemma still on her mind.

That night Chelby had a vivid dream about Mr. McIntosh. In her dream, she was somewhere in the woods. In a section of the woods, there was a massive gate in plain sight that stood higher than the trees that seemed to reach the clouds above, but she was unable to see how far the gate went around. In the distance, she could see people moving. As she approached, she noticed little kids inside crying next to a man. Once getting to the large gate, she saw those same children being pushed into a bottomless pit by that very man.

The man turned around to look at Chelby, and it was Mr. McIntosh staring back at her with a sly smirk. The cries from the children rang out as she shook the gate, yelling, "Stop, Help!" The young children were reaching for Chelby, but she could not get to them. She yelled, "STOP!" one more time and woke up in a sweat with her father standing right beside her in her room.

"Chelby, are you ok? Were you having a nightmare? Who were you whispering, stop to?" her father asked as he wiped her forehead full of sweat.

"It seemed so real, Dad. I'm ok, though," Chelby answered.

Marcus went to get Chelby some water from the kitchen. After giving it to her, he slowly kneeled beside her. "What happened baby, want to talk about it?" Marcus asked concernedly.

"Thank you, Daddy, for the water...and no, Dad, I'm ok, really," Chelby answered.

"Ok, baby. I'm right here if you need me. Try and go back to sleep," Chelby's father said.

Chelby closed her eyes and rolled over as Marcus prayed for her in a light whisper. Once Chelby went back to sleep, he left the room. "Goodnight, baby," Marcus said, leaving Chelby's room.

Chapter 2

Spark

The next day at school, during lunch, Chelby told Shyla bits and pieces of her vivid dream. Although somewhat embarrassed, she felt like she had to tell someone. Shyla made light of it, saying that she and Chelby could jump Mr. McIntosh whenever Chelby was ready. That made Chelby laugh as she thought about how nuts Shyla was. Then Chelby jokingly mentioned that Shyla's little, short self could barely reach his knees. "This may be true," Shyla said. "But I hit hard and run fast, so he's all yours after that!" They both busted out laughing.

Shyla is so crazy, Chelby thought.

* * *

A few days had passed, and it was time to meet with Cameron after school for the weekly tutoring session again. Chelby walked into the school library, eager to see him. Not only to help him with his work but, more importantly, to Chelby at least, ask more questions about Mr. McIntosh.

As she walked in, she saw Cameron in the same chair he was in on their first meeting and doodling just like he was before as well. "Hey Cameron, how was your day today?" Chelby asked.

"Hey, what's up Chelby, it was pretty good," Cameron replied.

"Wow, you have a lot of homework today Cameron," Chelby mentioned, looking over his work. "Let's get started."

As they worked on the math portion of Cameron's homework, she noticed that he would get down on himself any time he made a mistake.

Cameron sucked his teeth along with huffing and puffing every time he made an error. Chelby realized that she needed to ensure him that everyone made mistakes, that it was a part of learning.

"It's ok to mess up, Cameron. That's why I'm here. We can just erase or scratch it out and do it over again," Chelby explained. Cameron's eyes grew wide as he put down his pencil flat on the desk.

"No, no, no, Chelby, please don't erase. Mr. McIntosh hates seeing do-overs like that!" Cameron responded.

"So how do you fix your mistakes, Cameron, if you can't erase them?" Chelby asked.

"Mr. McIntosh just fixes it in the morning," Cameron replied.

"So, what happens if you do erase? Chelby asked.

Cameron began to look down and shake his head. "It's not good," Cameron murmured.

"Cameron, you can tell me, it's ok. What happens if you erase?" Chelby eagerly asked again.

Cameron took a deep breath and closed his eyes, then opened them back up before he answered. "He pinches us hard and makes us face the wall in the back of the class," Cameron replied in a low tone.

"What? Are you serious? Have you told your parents yet?" Chelby asked.

"No, he said that no one would believe a little kid, and if we told, we'd suffer the consequences," Cameron responded.

"Let's go tell the principal right now!" Chelby instructed as she began to get up.

"No, Chelby, all the teachers love him. He's right; no one will ever believe us," Cameron responded. Chelby slowly sat back down as Cameron explained more about what went on during Mr. Mcintosh's class.

Cameron told Chelby that Mr. McIntosh would throw students in the back of the class in a corner, standing up, face against the wall, where passing teachers couldn't see them. Cameron explained that Mr. McIntosh would tell the young students that no one would believe them if they didn't see it for themselves.

Cameron also explained that if he or his classmates forget how to spell their sight words on test day, Mr. McIntosh would go around the classroom to pinch them. He added that Mr. McIntosh hated to see eraser marks on their papers the most. Cameron told Chelby that Mr. McIntosh had even gone into one of his friend's backpacks and thrown out the student's snacks into the garbage, just for not following his rules properly.

Chelby couldn't believe her ears as Cameron described what went on in Mr. Mcintosh's class. She felt sorry for what Cameron, or any other student had to endure daily with him but angry that no one hadn't stop these awful acts from continuing as of yet.

Cameron lastly told Chelby that he didn't want his mother to get hurt over him. "What do you mean by that, Cameron?" Chelby asked.

"Well, he told us if we tell our parents about what happens in his class and he gets in trouble, that he would hurt our parents too," Cameron whimpered. Cameron explained that his father was no longer around and that his mother was his only parent. "If something happens to her, I wouldn't have any parents, and I love my mother so much," Cameron whispered.

Chelby took a big sigh as she rubbed Cameron's back. "Ok, Cameron, this will just be between you and me," Chelby replied. "Let's finish up so we can get out of here. It's starting to get a little late, ok," Chelby said. Cameron nodded his head as he continued with his work.

When Chelby went home, she kept what Cameron said to herself and chose not to tell her mother about it. Even the next day at school, when she saw Shyla, Chelby didn't tell her either. She felt like she had to figure this out on her own.

In the cafeteria, at lunch, Chelby and Shyla sat next to one another to both eat and talk. "What's up Chelby, glad it's Friday, right?" Shyla asked as she ate her food.

"I know, right, seemed like a long week," Chelby replied.

"Are you doing anything tomorrow?" Shyla asked.

"I don't think so, but Sunday, we're supposed to go bowling," Chelby replied.

"My mother closes the shop early on Sundays, and that's my father's only day off, so usually we do things on Sundays," Chelby explained.

"Oh, that's cool, real cool. I hope you all have fun," Shyla said.

"I might hit up the mall tomorrow. My mother can come pick you up if you like," Shyla added.

"Oh, that sounds cool, thanks. I'll tell my mother tonight for sure," Chelby responded.

Just at that moment, in the distance, Chelby seen food fly off the table to the left of her and onto the floor along with the tray. A boy who looked too big for the 6th grade was standing up on the opposite side from where the food landed. He was pointing and laughing with two of his friends, mimicking his gestures behind him. The boy whose food was now on the floor just looked down in shock.

"Billy Thompson, get over here!" a school aid shouted.

"No, you get over here!" Billy yelled back. Two other teachers, along with the lunch aid, approached Billy and his friends and escorted them out.

"Who was that?" Chelby asked Shyla.

"Oh, that fool, that's Billy; he stays in trouble," Shyla responded.

"Wow, I didn't see him last week, though," Chelby mentioned.

"Yeah, well, sometimes he's here, sometimes he's not. That kid has issues. He's always picking on somebody and getting in trouble somehow," Shyla responded.

Billy Thompson was a football player-sized student that towered over most students as well as some teachers. He had an intimidating look that most would fear. His hair was in cornrows that went straight back to his neck, which had colored rubber bands on the ends of it.

Chelby was used to seeing kids fight in her old school, but this was a little different for her. In her old school, students fought to prove they could fight without reasoning behind it most times. So, bullying students was something new to Chelby; that's why this Billy situation disturbed her even more than the random fighting did. Chelby felt it was outright disgusting to single out any student to belittle him or her for that person's amusement.

Later on, as she passed the main office heading to the bathroom, she saw Billy and his mother leaving the office. Billy's mother was smacking him in the back of his head and cursing at him as they left the school.

When going back to class, Chelby whispered to Shyla about what she just witnessed. "Oh yeah, Ms.

Thompson, she's even crazier than Billy. He must get it from her," Shyla murmured.

"Yeah, I guess so," Chelby replied as she shook her head.

The next day Chelby's mother allowed her to go to the mall with Shyla and her mother. They were having a great time going in and out of store's window shopping. Chelby lost count of how many times Shyla asked to buy something, and her mother would quickly shut her down each time.

Sitting at the food court while waiting for Shyla's mother to finish purchasing a new dress, Shyla and Chelby noticed Billy walking by with his friends. "Oh boy," they both said to one another at the same time.

Billy walked by a couple of random younger boys, stopped, and looked down at their food. The younger boys at the time were eating hotdogs and fries at Nathan's Famous. Billy snatched some of their fries and ate some. Then he smacked the rest of the food onto the floor along with the tray before running off. The friends that were with him followed behind Billy and ran off as well.

"So, I guess he just doesn't like people eating around him, huh?" Shyla asked.

"I guess not," Chelby replied. They both shook their heads.

Once Shyla's mother was finished shopping, they left the mall and headed home. After reaching home, Chelby's mother asked how her time at the mall went. "It was fun Mom, Shyla kept asking her mother to buy things, and every single time her mother refused," Chelby said. "It was too funny."

"That is funny," Chelby's mother agreed.

"Oh yeah, and this boy from my school was there too. I think he's a bully, Mom," Chelby mentioned. "Seems like he's always picking on somebody. Something is wrong with that boy!" she exclaimed.

"Well, there may truly be something wrong with him, Chelby. You never know. Sometimes kids act out when something is bothering them or if at home isn't right," Chelby's mother explained. "There's a lot of different reasons children act out with bad conduct. Usually, some bad things are going on in their lives, or they aren't treated with the love they need and deserve," Mia concluded.

"So, are you ready to get ya butt whooped in bowling tomorrow after we leave the shop?!" Chelby's mother asked.

"Well, first, I'm not losing, but yes, I can't wait!" Chelby responded.

"But I know Daddy is gonna probably beat us both," Chelby mentioned.

"Not if we trip him right before he bowls!" Mia responded. They both laughed, giving one another a high five. The next day while Chelby was at her mother's shop, Chelby would either help her mother and the customers if they needed her or look on with curiosity.

"Hey, Mom. Is it supposed to rain today? It's starting to get dark and cloudy outside?" Chelby asked her mother.

"No, baby, not that I know of, but it does look like it's about to rain," Mia replied.

"Listen, take the keys and put some of the things in the trunk, so if it does start to pour, we won't have to worry about it later," Chelby's mother instructed.

"Ok, Mom," Chelby replied.

Walking outside to the car, Chelby looked up at some of the dark clouds passing overhead. *Oh, yeah, it's about to pour*, she thought to herself. She closed the trunk and pressed the button to lock the door. Walking back into the salon to give the keys back to her mother, Chelby noticed that some customers were looking outside at the darkening clouds.

She thought, luckily, the shop closed early on Sundays so she and her mother might beat the rain. As the ladies left the shop, Chelby's mother would wish them a safe trip home and a goodnight.

They would all say thank you and give compliments to their hairdresser as they left out. Once all the customers were out of the building, Mia and one of her employees counted the drawer for the night. After the ladies situated the money, the employee left for the night and left behind Chelby and her mother. Both Mia and Chelby looked up at the same time because of a slight rumble overhead.

"Hey, you heard that?" Chelby mentioned.

"Sure did. Let's hurry up and wash your hair so I can put you under this dryer, and we can leave. I hate driving in the rain," Mia demanded.

Chelby wasn't concerned about the rain as much as her mother was. She loved getting her hair washed and was eager to do so.

The roar of the thunder got louder as it began to rain outside. "Woah! That was close," Mia said after watching a visible lightning bolt strike right outside the glass doors. "Ok, Chelby, sit under this dryer, and I'll be right back. You need a magazine to read?" Mia asked.

"Yes, please, can you pass me that Shape book," Chelby asked.

"Sure, honey," Chelby's mother replied.

Mia walked over to get the magazine as flashes of bright light were filling the shop, startling Mia some. Loud booming thunder sounded off seconds after the flashes of light, vibrating through the building louder each time.

Mia went to the back of the shop to check something when an enormous flash of light, followed by a thunderous boom, struck almost simultaneously. The sound made Mia jump then fall. The noise sounded like it broke the glass of the front doors. As she gathered herself, opening her eyes and removing her hands from her ears, Mia turned around on her side to see Chelby stretched out in the middle of the floor.

Mia could view the magazine on the floor inches from Chelby's hand with pieces of it burning. One of

Chelby's shoes was off on the opposite side of the shop as well.

"Chelby... CHELBY!" her mother screamed as she abruptly crawled to her. Chelby was not responsive as Mia called her name. Mia got back up to get to her phone and dove back to Chelby as she called 911, crying and screaming. The person on the other end could barely make out what Mia was saying. But she did make out the word "burns" and something about Chelby and lightning. So, the operator traced the call sending fire trucks and EMTs to the scene.

Mia began to plead with God that Chelby would be ok as she held her in her arms. The electricity left half of Chelby's hair and scalp burnt along with her neck and forearm. Most of the damage was on the same side where Chelby was holding the magazine. Since Chelby rolled up her sleeves as she sat under the dryer, Mia noticed that the very same forearm now had a small mark on it.

It was as if Chelby's veins on her arm were highlighted in a streaky formation similar to how a tree looked. The mark also had a slight faint glow to it, like a 3D-lit tattoo of sorts.

Chelby still had yet to take a breath, and as minutes passed, that seemed to be a lifetime for Mia. Mia began to panic and started to perform CPR to get Chelby to breathe again. Mia could hear the sirens surrounding her as smoke began to suffocate the shop. The fireman rushed in, carrying both Chelby and her worrisome mother out.

Once the EMTs got a hold of Chelby, their concern was to get her back breathing again. "Please save my daughter!" Mia begged through her flowing tears.

The EMTs were able to get Chelby breathing again. With an oxygen mask placed on Chelby's face and her mother on the side of her, they were rushed to the hospital. After reaching the hospital, the nurses could see Chelby was in pain, moaning, and screaming back and forth. Once in the ER, the doctors worked on Chelby immediately.

While in the ambulance, Mia called Chelby's father to inform him of the tragic news. Marcus must have flown to the hospital because he arrived not too long after Chelby and her mother had. Marcus found where Chelby and Mia were and went straight to them in a frantic rush.

After finally reaching where they were, Marcus and Mia embraced as they have never held each other before. Mia was crying uncontrollably as Marcus tried to console her by holding her close to his chest. "Where is she?" Marcus asked at a hurried pace.

"She's in that room right there," Mia replied, pointing towards the room Chelby was in.

"Can we go in?" Marcus asked. Just as he asked, a doctor came out to speak with both parents.

"Hello Mr. And Mrs. William's. I'm Dr. Miller," The doctor said, shaking Marcus and Mia's hands. "I'm sorry to inform you, but your daughter has suffered 3rd-degree burns on her scalp, neck, back, arms, and legs. She was in a lot of pain, so we gave her something for that. It says here that your daughter's heart had stopped back at the shop, but she is miraculously in stable condition right now," Dr. Miller explained, as he viewed the chart in his hands.

Mia burst into tears once hearing the information given by the doctor. "Chelby is weak right now, but parents, you have a strong little girl right there. She's a fighter," Dr. Miller continued. "She is on an I.V. for now, and we are monitoring her heart rate, which is slowly normalizing," he added. "Mrs. Williams, were you with her at the time of the incident? Was your daughter electrocuted somehow?" Dr. Miller, puzzling, asked.

47

"I think... she was struck by lightning," Mia responded.

"Lightning? Was she outside?" the doctor asked curiously.

"No, she was in my shop during the thunderstorm under the dryer. There was a flash, then a boom, and when I turned around, she was stretched out on the floor," Mia struggled to explain.

"Ok, Mom, I know it's hard for you right now, so no more questions for now," Dr. Miller said.

Marcus briefly looked up then back at Dr. Miller with tears swelling up in his eyes. "Thank you, Doctor, but can we see her now?" Marcus whispered, gathering himself.

"Yes, you can, but please do not touch her right now," the doctor instructed.

As Chelby's parents entered the room, they both began to cry. Seeing all of the monitors going and tubes attached to Chelby was devastating to view. As they got closer, they could see that half of Chelby's hair was burnt and damaged. Her neck and arms had a black, reddish, leathery look to them. The texture of her burnt skin looked similar to if a person put a lighter underneath a leather belt and held it there.

Marcus noticed the highlighted tree mark on his daughter's arm as well. "What is this monitor for, Doctor," Marcus asked, pointing to one of many monitors in the room.

"This is to follow her brain patterns Mr. Williams," Dr. Miller replied. "To be honest with you, Mr. Williams, being directly struck with as much voltage as in a lightning bolt will leave most with brain damage or in a coma. So, we are paying close attention to Chelby, just monitoring everything we can right now. Also, nerve damage is possible, and unfortunately, her hair may never grow back as well. But her vital signs are normalizing, which is most important right now," Dr. Miller explained.

"Ok, Doctor, thank you," Marcus replied.

"Stay by your daughter's side. She needs your love right now," Dr. Miller responded.

Both Marcus and Mia nodded their heads as the doctor went to check the monitors.

"I can't believe this happened to our baby," Mia whispered to her husband.

"She's going to be ok babe, she's going to be alright," Marcus replied, rubbing Mia's back.

Between the tragic event that just took place and the medicines giving to Chelby for the pain, Chelby was sound asleep. She dreamt vividly of what just happened to her at the shop, and right as she got struck by lightning in her dream, she woke up gasping for air.

"Hey baby, we're right here," Marcus mumbled. Mia, with tears in her eyes, was unable to speak at that time. Chelby opened the palm of her hand to say hi.

"Hey, Daddy," Chelby groggily replied. "I'm so thirsty," Chelby whispered. "And my skin feels so tight, too."

"Baby, you have burns all over your body. You were..." Marcus hung his head as he struggled to finish.

"I'm so sorry Chelby, I can't believe this happened!" Mia said. "This is all my fault... I-I should have taken you off the dryer when I saw, I... I didn't know..." Mia struggled to form the words to complete her thought.

"I'll be ok, Mom, don't worry," Chelby softly replied. Chelby drifted off to sleep again right after responding to her mother.

"Can I have a word with y'all outside Mr. and Mrs. Williams?" Dr. Miller asked. "She needs to rest anyway," he added.

Once all three were in the hallway, Dr. Miller began to speak again. "So, parents, the good news, actually great news, is that Chelby's heart rate is almost back to normal. Now, her brain patterns are kind of all over the place but it's nothing to worry about," Dr. Miller exclaimed.

He took a deep breath before beginning his following sentence. Chelby's parent's faces showed more concern than before. "So, your daughter, as you now know, have suffered severe 3rd-degree burns throughout her body, Mr. and Mrs. Williams. The part of her scalp that was struck we don't believe will grow hair again. Too much damage has occurred. Now on her neck, back, arms, and legs, it's more than likely she'll suffer nerve damage. We suggest doing a surgical procedure called skin grafting," Dr. Miller continued.

"The purpose of the procedure is to replace the damaged skin and can take a couple of hours to complete."

"My God!" Mia pleaded.

"Do you suggest this, Doctor?" Marcus asked.

"I do, Mr. Williams. It's a simple procedure that can and should help your daughter at this time," Dr. Miller replied.

Chelby's parents took a moment to talk it over between the two of them, and after a couple of minutes, agreed to proceed with the surgery.

"Ok, Doctor, my wife and I agreed to go through with it. Please take care of our daughter, Doctor, please," Marcus begged.

"She is in great hands," Dr. Miller replied. "You are going to have to sign some paperwork, and I will call you back when we are about to start the surgery in a few hours," Dr. Miller said. Marcus shook the doctor's hand as he entered Chelby's room again while Mia held onto the bed with a longing look once reentering.

"It's ok, baby, let's go outside," Marcus whispered. Mia blew a kiss to Chelby and whispered thank you to the doctor as she exited with Marcus.

Several hours had passed, which seemed like days to the Williams couple. They both took turns pacing the hospital floors as one would stay back outside Chelby's room, while the other would peek in every chance given. Then suddenly, a doctor was called to Chelby's room. Seconds later, two more followed, then another. Mia stood up and asked a doctor what was happening. The doctor was very short in replying, "One-second, ma'am!"

Several minutes had passed when Dr. Miller had called Chelby's parents back inside the room. Just from first glance, it seemed like there was a doctor at each monitor, looking at reports and going over them. "What's wrong doctor, is there something wrong with Chelby?" Marcus asked. Dr. Miller slowly inhaled before letting out a breath as his right hand went over his mouth and goatee.

"I want to show you something," Dr. Miller said as he walked Chelby's parents to the monitors. "You see this, that's her heart rate and pressure. It has drastically changed from mediocre to great. Her brain patterns are still a little erratic, but that could be because of vivid dreaming," Dr. Miller explained. "But I need you to come take a look at her," Dr. Miller said as he walked them over to Chelby.

Chelby's parents walked over to her with apprehension. "Mom, do you see anything different?" Dr. Miller asked, looking at Mia.

Mia looked down in shock. She paused before responding. "It...it doesn't look as bad as before," Mia shockingly responded.

"Doesn't look as bad? Ms. Williams, the way Chelby looks right now in comparison to before, is as if she had a long day at the beach," Dr. Miller replied.

"Doctor, I don't understand," Marcus responded as he looked Chelby over.

"Look at her neck and arms. Look at her legs, at her scalp. Your daughter for sure didn't look like this when she came in," Dr. Miller mentioned.

"So, what happened to her then Doc? Did y'all do the procedure or something while we sat and waited outside?" Marcus asked.

"Of course not, Mr. Williams. We would've told you exactly when we would start because we would've had to take her to another room. The severity of her burns is minor right now and nowhere near what somebody struck by lightning should have. I'm not a religious man myself, Mr. Williams, but a higher power had to be involved!" Dr. Miller looked at Chelby and then back to her parents. "I've never seen anything like this recovery, in so short of time, in all my years with medicine," Dr. Miller admittedly said. "Although she's still out of it, once she wakes up, I believe we'll be able to discharge her," Dr. Miller concluded.

Mia thanked God as she hugged her husband and then thanked the doctor and staff.

"No problem, Mrs. Williams, I told you she was a strong girl!" Dr. Miller responded.

"We know, Doctor, and thank you," Mr. Williams replied emotionally.

"I will write you a list of how to treat the burns she has, and you are free to go," Dr. Miller said.

"Oh, thank you, thank you," Marcus and Mia replied simultaneously.

"Y'all are more than welcome. Just take care of your little girl. She's special!" Dr. Miller responded as he left the room.

As soon as Chelby was up and able to leave, the Williams family got their belongings and paperwork from the hospital to head home. Marcus double backed to the room Chelby was in to make sure he nor Mia left anything behind. Although Marcus was both emotionally drained and physically fatigued from the night's tragic events, he still made sure to kiss Mia and Chelby before leaving to head home in his car. Chelby strolled to her mother's car, unaware of the strain and worry placed on her parents at this time.

Once in Mia's car, Chelby asked about her mother's shop. "What about your salon Mom, was it burned down?" Chelby asked.

"I don't know, Chelby, we'll worry about that later. I just thank God you are ok," Mia responded as she pulled off to head home.

Mia and Marcus slept soundly that night, knowing that their beloved only child was safe with them at home. Chelby wasn't as lucky. She had a restless night. Dreaming about the lightning on several occasions, she would suddenly wake up but then turn over to go back to sleep again. Every time, she would wake up rubbing her forearm where the tree-like mark sat. For some odd reason, it pained her and bothered her the most.

A couple of weeks had passed when her friend Shyla came to visit her at home. They hadn't seen one another since the tragic night at the salon, so they both were eager to catch up. Shyla's mother, Ms. Natasha Baxter, drove Shyla to the Williams apartment, and Ms. Baxter came inside and stayed to check on Mia as well.

"What's up Chelby, how are you feeling?" Shyla asked as she hugged Chelby entering the Williams apartment.

Hugging Shyla back, Chelby responded, "Hey Shyla, I'm doing ok, thanks. I'm still a little sore, but for the most part, I feel pretty good," Chelby admitted.

Shyla looked Chelby up and down, confused. "Hey Chelby, thought you told me that half your hair was burned off when we spoke over the phone last week? I don't see much of a difference except for those scabs around your forehead."

"Yeah, it was. I don't know. It just started to grow back as the burns healed up, I guess," Chelby replied.

"In two weeks? That's crazy?!" Shyla shouted.

"Yeah, I know, it is kinda crazy, but I'm just happy that it's growing back, you know," Chelby responded.

"So, what's up with your mother's shop? I walked by there the other day, and It looks like they started to fix it back up already," Shyla asked.

"Yeah, my mother called the insurance people a few days after it happened, and they got right to it," Chelby replied.

"Think my mother said it should be back up and running in a couple more weeks," Chelby added.

"Oh, that's cool!" Shyla responded.

"So let me see this tattoo thing you told me about," Shyla mentioned. Chelby slowly rolled up the sleeve of her sweater to show off the tree mark. "Oh, that's cute. I actually thought it'd be bigger than that. You can barely see it," Shyla said.

"Yeah, I guess you're right, but It bothers me the most, though," Chelby admitted.

"What you mean?" Shyla asked.

"It itches a lot, and sometimes I have sharp pains in that area, too," Chelby explained.

"Probably because it's healing, that's why," Shyla replied. "You coming back to school tomorrow, right? Ms. Spiegal and some of the students have been asking about you."

"Yeah, I'll be back tomorrow for sure. I miss school too," Chelby responded. The two continued to catch up until Ms. Baxter called from the living room for Shyla to get ready to leave. The four ladies exchanged hugs as Shyla, and her mother left the apartment.

Later that night, after dinner, Chelby got ready to get her hair done by her mother for school the following day.

"So, are you excited to get back to school tomorrow, baby?" Mia asked.

"Yes, definitely, plus I've been kinda bored here at home too," Chelby replied.

"Hey, Mom. Can you give me crown braids for tomorrow? I saw it in this magazine, and it looked pretty on the lady?" Chelby asked.

"Sure, baby. I swear I still can't believe your hair has almost completely grown back, and this fast at that, it's incredible. This whole thing is just crazy to me, your fast recovery included, but I thank God you are ok," Mia admitted.

Chelby and Mia would converse about random things while Mia was finishing up with Chelby's hair. This time, Chelby brought two small handheld mirrors to see how her hair came out without leaving the living room. One thick twisted braid that started a few inches over one ear went around to the other ear in a U formation. The part in Chelby's hair was slightly curved, which gave the crown braid a unique look to it. Mia also put small gold-plated beads throughout Chelby's crown braid to provide it with a royalty effect and to add a little flavor to it as well.

"Wow, Mom, it looks better than the picture in the magazine does. Thanks so much!" Chelby exclaimed.

"Welcome, baby, anytime," Mia replied. Once done, Mia got up to wash the dishes as Chelby got off the floor onto the couch to watch TV. A few minutes after Mia finished braiding Chelby's hair, Chelby's forearm began to itch. First a little, but then noticeably a lot. Mia looked over to where Chelby sat to see what was bothering her.

"What's wrong baby, is your arm itching again?" Mia asked.

Scratching profusely, Chelby responded, "Yeah, Mom, it's itching, a-a lot!" Then Chelby began to wince as if in some sort of pain. She stood up and screamed while holding her forearm. "Mommy, it hurts!"

Before Mia could get to Chelby from the kitchen, Chelby grabbed the arm of the couch and pushed it clear down the long hallway in one motion. She knocked over her bike, a lamp, and two chairs in the process, leaving them both standing there in amazement.

Both Chelby and Mia were speechless at what took place, but something else quickly drew their attention. "Baby...your arm!" Mia shockingly said, pointing towards Chelby's arm.

At that very moment, Chelby felt her arm seem to sort of vibrate and pulse like a heartbeat. As she looked down, she noticed that she could see a slight glow under her sweater. She rolled up the sleeve, and the tree-like bruise that was now embedded on Chelby's arm like a tattoo seemed to glow with white and bluish light.

Although the glow was faint, it was noticeable by both Mia and Chelby. After a few moments, Chelby finally found the words to speak.

"Mom, what's going on?" Chelby whispered to her mother.

"Chelby, I don't know," Mia whispered back. As fast as the glow and sensations began, it had stopped. The two of them looked around at one another, not knowing what to do next.

"Baby, I don't know what just happened, but let's try and get this place cleaned up a little as I try and figure this out," Mia instructed. Chelby nodded her head in agreement. After briefly cleaning up, they now had the task of pushing the couch back down the hall to where it was initially. A job indeed, it was a struggle for Marcus and his brother to get the sofa there in the first place. "Ok, baby, let's try and push this couch back," Mia said. Chelby took one corner and Mia the other.

"On 3," Mia instructed. "1... 2... 3!" Mia and Chelby counted together before they began to push. Chelby had her head down towards her feet as Mia pushed, head up to see where she was going. A glimpse of something caught the corner of Mia's eye. Once distracted, she felt compelled to stop pushing. Mia noticed Chelby's arm starting to glow again, but even more bizarre than that, Chelby was moving the couch by herself.

"Chelby?" Mia shouted. "Huh?" Chelby responded, looking back at her mother confusingly. Chelby didn't notice, but when she looked back, she took one hand off and now was pushing the couch with just one hand. Once realizing, Chelby stopped dead in her tracks with a puzzled look on her face.

"Whoa, how did I just do that, Mom?" Chelby asked.

"Baby, I have no idea," her mother walked over to her with both hands up and a nervous grin on her face and said. "How do you feel? Do you feel ok?" Mia asked.

"I feel fine, Mom. I feel regular," Chelby replied.

"Well, have you been taken steroids or something because you just moved that heavy couch with one hand down the hall without even noticing?" Mia joked.

"No, Mom, of course not. I don't know how that just happened," Chelby responded, with a small but nervous chuckle.

They both finished cleaning up, not understanding how to grasp what just took place. "Are you gonna tell Dad about what happened?" Chelby asked.

"Yes, of course, I am. I just have to figure out what to tell him, " Mia said, still completely confused. Mia kissed, then hugged Chelby, and told her to get some rest, and Chelby did just that.

Chapter 3

Bullies Young and Old

On Chelby's first day back to school, she was greeted with open arms. Most of the school heard about what happened at the salon and was happy to see that she was alright. Her classmates made her feel good when they saw her that day—most running up to greet her with hugs and some to express their concerns. Shyla kept them posted on Chelby's miraculous recovery. At lunch, Shyla and Chelby sat next to one another as usual.

Their conversation was interrupted when Billy walked over to sit at the same table they were at, just on the opposite end. They both let out a deep sigh once they saw him. The students, including Chelby and Shyla, tried to ignore his presence at the table, but he made sure everyone noticed. He started messing with one of the student's bags and clothes and began calling that student disrespectful names.

The boy slowly got up to walk and sit at another table as Billy's antics continued. He sat back down at a table directly next to Chelby and Shyla. Billy didn't hesitate to follow the student and that's when Shyla spoke up to say something.

"Hey, just leave him alone, Billy," Shyla demanded of him.

"Mind your business, small fry, nobody asked you," Billy replied. "He got up and left the table already, leave him be!" Chelby said sternly.

"Oh, you got something to say, new girl?" Billy asked with a smirk on his face as he approached Chelby at the end of the lunch table. Billy placed both his hands on the table directly in front of Chelby's face and crouched over to yell at her.

"Listen, new girl, I don't care about you getting burned or your mother's stupid shop burning to the ground. You stay out of my business. You got it!" Billy demanded. As Billy began to say this, Chelby's arm began to itch, but she nor any other student noticed the faint glow under her shirt's long sleeves.

"Get out of my face, boy!" Chelby screamed. As she yelled, she pushed Billy in his chest simultaneously. Billy flew over the table behind him and slid underneath the table next to that one. From the impact of Billy's body sliding backward into the table, food and drinks from above fell all over him. Anyone who walked by the scene could see the school lunch spotted all over Billy's head, shirt, and pants. The students that witnessed this couldn't believe their eyes, and all seemed to say, "OOOUUU!" in a low whisper at once.

Shyla looked at Chelby as Chelby looked back at her. Both of their mouths were left open in shock. Chelby got up seconds later and ran right into the girl's bathroom. Shyla took a quick look at Billy, giggled, then ran to the girl's bathroom moments after, following behind Chelby. School aids and teachers rushed to the commotion as both Chelby and Shyla huddled in the bathroom. Once inside, Shyla looked at Chelby from head to toe before she spoke.

"Yo, what was that?!" Shyla asked. "That was one heck off a push, girl," she added.

"I don't know, but is Billy, ok? "Chelby asked. "I just got so upset."

"Well, last I saw of Billy, he was on the floor covered in school lunch," Shyla replied, giggling.

As they were talking, teachers rushed to the girl's bathroom to order the girls out. "Ms. Chelby Williams, if you are in there, can you come out, please? We have to talk to you?" one teacher ordered.

Both girls came out and were escorted to the main office. Shyla was able to go back to class, while Chelby had to stay back and talk to the assistant principal. Billy was already in the main office, still wiping down his clothes. You could almost see steam coming up from the top of his head. As Chelby walked in, he looked at her with piercing eyes that left little doubt of forgiveness.

"Billy, are you ok? I'm so sorry about that," Chelby sincerely asked.

Billy looked over his clothes while brushing down his pants before responding. "Yeah, I'm good new girl, you won't be, though!" he replied in a low voice.

"I truly am sorry, Billy," Chelby added.

Just then, Ms. Bell, the assistant principal, came from the back of the office to meet with both Chelby and Billy. "Billy, you again, what did you do this time?" she asked.

Before Billy could respond, she cut him off and directed her attention to Chelby.

"Chelby Williams, correct? Are you the little girl that was saved from the fire a few weeks back?" Ms. Bell asked. Chelby nodded her head, yes. "Oh, I'm so sorry to hear about you and your mother, but glad to see that you are alright. Unfortunately, I am going to have to call her to come down here to help mediate this situation along with Billy's mother. Fighting is prohibited at this school, no exceptions," Ms. Bell concluded.

Both parents were called and notified of the situation and asked to come up to the school to help mediate before the school took further actions. Once each of the children's parents arrived, they were asked to sit in Ms. Bell's office along with their child.

"How are you, Mrs. Williams? I'm Ms. Bell. Thank you for coming in on such short notice," Ms. Bell said as she shook Chelby's mother's hand.

"No problem at all. I'm fine, thank you, nice to meet you as well," Mia responded.

"Good morning Ms. Thompson. I'm sorry I had to ask you to come on such short notice as well," Ms. Bell added.

"Uh-huh… I have to get back to work, so what did this boy do this time?" Billy's mother responded as she stared at Billy angrily.

"Well, I'll let the young adults speak on it. Ladies first, Chelby, you have the floor," Ms. Bell instructed, pointing to Chelby to speak.

"Well, Billy was picking on another student, and I asked him to leave him alone. He then got into my face and said some mean disrespectful things to me. I got upset and overreacted and pushed him. He fell, and I got up and ran to the bathroom. I'm really embarrassed with myself that I didn't control my anger before pushing him, " Chelby explained. Mia looked at Chelby with a shocked look on her face as her daughter was speaking. Both parents tried to interject, but Ms. Bell cut them off.

"One second, parents. Allow Billy to speak, please," Ms. Bell said, now pointing to Billy.

"Yeah, I was just playing with the boy when the new girl stepped in and told me to leave him alone. I walked over to her, and she pushed me, and I tripped and fell, " Billy concluded.

"So why am I even here? Billy was hit first. It was the girl's fault!" Ms. Thompson responded.

"First off, her name is Chelby, and she never fights with anyone, so she was most likely provoked and pushed your son to defend herself," Mia replied.

"Ladies, ladies, please! We are here to come to a common ground and not fight about who's fault it is," Ms. Bell said.

Once both mothers calmed down some, they agreed to disagree about the situation. Ms. Bell reminded them both that the school did not tolerate fighting under any circumstances. Both parents agreed with that, and both Chelby and Billy were sent back to their classes with only a warning never to do this again as the parents left the school.

When Chelby returned to her class, Shyla looked at Chelby eagerly, waiting to hear about everything.

"I'll tell you later, Shyla, but you're right. Billy's mother is nuts!" Chelby whispered.

Shyla replied, "Told ya!"

Later that night, Mia and Chelby discussed more of what happened at school. "Chelby, you pushed that big boy like that?" Mia asked.

"It was worse. He flew over the table and underneath another one, Mom!" Chelby explained.

"What in the world? How could you do that? He's double your size!" Mia asked.

Chelby shrugged her shoulders as she looked down at her arm. "You think it was the fire, Chelby?" Mia hesitantly asked.

"I don't know, Mom. What else could it be?" Chelby replied. "What did the people say of how the fire started, again?" Chelby asked.

"The same as we told you, baby. There was a small unnoticeable leak over the dryers, which caused some sort of electrical short in the dryer. Once the lightning hit the building, it caused a fire to spark while you were under drying your hair. They say it was a miracle you survived," Chelby's mother concluded.

"It has to be related then Mom," Chelby replied.

"To tell you the truth, I've seen with my own eyes that mark on your arm glow, and your sudden freakish strength doesn't make any sense at all. Let's see what your father says about it when he gets home tonight," Mia responded.

Mia allowed Chelby to stay up to talk with her father about everything. The fight, the miraculous recovery, and whatever was happening to Chelby needed to be discussed. Once Marcus got home and settled in, they sat at the dinner table to speak on these puzzling occurrences.

"You pushed that couch across the house, Chelby, and the boy fight; this is all true?" Marcus asked. Chelby nodded her head, yes. Marcus rubbed his forehead slowly and slid down his face with his hand. "I-I don't know what to make of all this... and that mark on your arm, your mother said it glows?" Marcus asked.

"Yes, but not all the time," Chelby responded.

"Did it glow today during the fight with the boy?" Marcus questioned.

"I don't know, I was too upset to notice," Chelby replied.

"Well, we need to keep this thing to ourselves until I can figure out what to do next, ok?" Marcus stated.

They all agreed, hugged, and went to their rooms to go to bed for the night.

Later on, that week at school, Chelby met up with Cameron to tutor him. They hadn't seen one another since the tragic events at Mia's salon. Cameron sat where he typically sits and was doodling as he usually does as well.

"Hey, Cameron!" Chelby excitedly said, walking into the library. Cameron jumped out of his seat to run and hug Chelby.

"Hey Chelby, I missed you. Are you ok?" Cameron asked.

"Yes, I'm good, Cameron," Chelby replied as she hugged him back.

They both sat down to begin Cameron's homework. "I heard you were in a fire Chelby, are you sure you're ok now?" Cameron asked.

"Yes, I'm much better, thank you, Cameron. So how have school been?" Chelby asked.

"Pretty good, but Mr. McIntosh is still so mean to us," Cameron mumbled.

"Oh, is he, don't worry, Cameron, I'm gonna figure this out," Chelby responded.

As Cameron began to read the book he chose for that day, Chelby thought about confronting Mr. McIntosh. *I should just hold him down and tell him to stop hurting his students*, she thought to herself. *Nah, that won't work. Maybe I should just push him like I did Billy, but that probably won't stop him either. Plus, everybody would know theirs something different about me too.*

She couldn't figure out what to do. Leaving the library with Cameron, Chelby happened to see Billy leaving the Principal's office.

"Hey, look who it is. It's the new girl," Billy said with a slick tone. "What you doing? Babysitting?"

"I'm not a baby, and her name is Chelby!" Cameron shouted.

Chelby smiled at little Cameron, trying to take up for her. "I'm tutoring and helping him with his homework, Billy. You know that school program, but why are you still here?" Chelby questioned.

"Still minding my business, huh, new girl? By the way, that was a pretty good push the other day. I must have slipped or something," Billy mentioned. Billy tried to change the subject on why he came from the main office at that time of day.

"Once again, I'm sorry, Billy. I lost control of myself," Chelby admitted. "But you have to stop bullying everybody. It's not right. If you continue, no one will ever like you, maybe they'll pretend to, but that'll only be because they are scared of you," Chelby added.

"I was just messing with that little guy at lunch that day, but I don't care if they like me or not. I'll rather they fear me!" Billy explained. "About that lucky push, it's all good new girl, just don't let it happen again!" He said as he went downstairs to exit the school.

Chelby shook her head at Billy's stubbornness and unwillingness to change as she and Cameron began to leave the school.

A few days had passed, and it was once again time for Chelby to meet up with Cameron for tutoring after school. Chelby asked Shyla to come with her to Mr. McIntosh's class before lunch. The young students mistreated by Mr. McIntosh stayed on her mind, and Chelby felt compelled to do something about it. Chelby didn't tell Shyla exactly why she wanted to see Mr. McIntosh but expressed that she needed to talk to him briefly. Shyla agreed to walk with her but mentioned that she was starving and asked her to hurry up so they wouldn't miss lunch.

Once outside of Mr. McIntosh's class, they both looked in and saw him grading student papers. Shyla stood outside as Chelby walked in. She felt confident and brave as she continued walking towards where Mr. McIntosh sat.

"Yes, do you need something, young lady?" Mr. McIntosh asked Chelby as she approached him.

"Yes, I'm Chelby Williams, and I wanted to talk to you about the students in your class," Chelby explained.

At that moment, Mr. McIntosh's face turned from looking confused to an expression of annoyance. "I'm listening," Mr. McIntosh replied. Chelby didn't want to mention Cameron's name because of fear that he may be singled out and mistreated more later on.

"Well, Mr. McIntosh, I've seen you mistreat some of your students before, and I'm pretty sure you do it all the time," Chelby admitted. "Nobody should be mistreated, especially not by a teacher, because most students look up to their teachers," Chelby continued. "I need you to stop, or I will let someone know about what's going on," she added.

"So, you know this to be a fact, huh?" Mr. McIntosh asked. "You've seen me do this and that, and you know about that and this… is that so?" He looked Chelby up and down before he continued. "You don't know anything, little girl, plus who is going to believe you over me?" Mr. Mcintosh asked. "You have a lot of nerve coming in my class with all these questions and accusations. It would be best if you left now before I make you go!" Mr. Mcintosh concluded.

As he said this, he stood up and pointed to the door as Chelby's fist clenched. She wanted to throw him over his desk but quickly thought otherwise. "I'm going to leave your classroom Mr. McIntosh, but this is not the end of this," Chelby said. "What you are doing is wrong, and it will stop. I'm going to make sure of that!" Chelby added as she walked out of the classroom to Shyla.

"Man, what happened in there, Chelby?" Shyla asked.

"Nothing Shyla, let's hurry up and get to lunch," Chelby replied.

A couple of days had passed since Chelby's war of words with Mr. McIntosh, and it was now Sunday, which was family day for the Williams'. Chelby and her mother were having breakfast at Denny's, which was not too far from their new apartment. They both awaited Marcus, who was currently at the gym finishing up to head to them.

"How's your food?" Mia asked.

"Everything is great!" Chelby admitted, mumbling with food still in her mouth. "I just love this place," Chelby continued.

"I know you do. So, how's school been since the situation with Billy?" Mia asked.

"It's been good, I've seen Billy since then, and everything seems to be ok," Chelby responded.

"Did anybody notice or say anything about what happened that day?" Mia asked.

"No, not anybody, not even Shyla, and she would have said something if she did," Chelby replied.

"Oh, thank goodness, that's the last thing we need," Mia admitted.

Chelby's father walked in and kissed both Chelby and Mia before sitting down. Once he was seated, Marcus immediately picked up the menu wishing the food was already in front of him.

"Hey Dad, I have something I want to tell you," Chelby said.

"Sure, baby, is everything alright?" Marcus asked.

Chelby told her father all about Mr. McIntosh and how he mistreated the younger students in school. Marcus was surprised that Chelby kept this from him but was worried about the young students as well.

"So Chelby, are you absolutely sure you saw him mistreat the younger kids?" Marcus asked.

"Yes, Daddy, I'm one hundred percent sure!" Chelby responded. Chelby continued by letting her father know what happened when she went to talk to Mr. McIntosh as well.

"Was he disrespectful towards you, Chelby?" Marcus asked.

"No, he wasn't Dad, but he definitely was annoyed that I confronted him about the students," Chelby responded.

Chelby was taught by her parents always to be honest with them, even if she felt uncomfortable doing so. She trusted that even when she wanted to keep things to herself, being forthcoming with the truth would work out in the end somehow because of the love her parents had for her. Chelby knew they truly wanted the best for her. She felt all parents should want this for their children.

"I swear, you're a brave little girl, by the way, once we leave here, I have something in the car for you," Marcus mentioned.

After they left the restaurant, Chelby rushed to get to her father's car parked right outside. She saw a bag in the backseat but couldn't make out what was in it. Once both her parents reached the car, her father hit the button to open it. "What is it Dad, what is it?" Chelby impatiently asked.

"Open up the bag and look for yourself," Marcus replied.

Chelby did and to her delight she saw that her father had replaced her favorite purple hood that was damaged in the fire. "Wow, this is nice!" Chelby said. The new one was a purple and blue dip-dye cinched-hem pullover hoodie he got from Old Navy. Chelby just had to try it on right then and there, store tag and all. She reached up and gave her father a big hug and kiss. "I just love it, Dad. You're the best!" Chelby excitedly said.

"I'm glad you like it, baby. I love you," Marcus replied.

Mia drove home by herself as Chelby went with her father in his car. On the ride back home, they discussed many things. One topic, in particular, was about this new, weird ability that Chelby now possessed. They both still were having trouble making sense of it.

"So, your mother thinks what is happening to you somehow is connected to what happened in the shop, huh?" Marcus asked.

"Yeah, Dad, that's the only thing we could come up with," Chelby responded.

"Your mother might be right, Chelby, but we just have to make sure to keep this topic to ourselves," Marcus exclaimed.

Once all three reached home and settled in, they all went off to do their own thing. Mia went to start Sunday dinner, Chelby went to take care of her homework, and Marcus took a long nap. As Chelby was finishing up her homework, Mia asked if Chelby wanted to play Jenga before dinner was ready. "Of course, Mom, I'll be done with everything in a second," Chelby answered from her room.

"Ok, good, come and get me when you're finished," Mia replied. The two played for several minutes as the food continued to cook. Every once in a while, Mia would get up to check on it. They traded wins back and forth as Marcus slowly crept out of the bedroom from his long nap.

"Oh, you must have just smelled the food cooking, huh?" Mia jokingly asked Marcus.

Marcus gave a big stretch with both arms over his head before saying, "I sure did. What are you making?" Chelby smiled at her father, knowing that the food smell truly did wake him up.

"Chicken quesadillas with fries and onion rings," Mia replied as she got up to head to the kitchen. "Come on, Chelby, time to eat. I'll finish beating you later," Mia said.

"Yeah, right, Mom, it's tied first of all, and I was just about to win," Chelby responded with a smirk on her face. Mia fixed the plates as Chelby and Marcus sat down at the table to eat. Once all three were sitting at the table, Marcus reminded Mia and Chelby to pray over the food. While Marcus said a quick prayer to bless the food, Chelby and Mia bowed their heads with their eyes closed and began to eat. Afterward, Marcus washed the dishes as Chelby sat on the floor in front of the couch, waiting for Mia to do her hair.

Marcus didn't wash dishes often, but on Sundays, he always did. "Hey Chelby, you know who

Rhianna is, right? I saw this cute hairstyle she had that gave me an idea to do for you," Mia shouted, coming from her bedroom into the living room.

"Yeah, of course, Mom. How did she have her hair?" Chelby eagerly asked.

"It was a cute bun up top with bangs coming down over her eyes, simple but cute," Mia responded.

"Sounds real cute. Let's do it!" Chelby excitedly replied. As Mia began to do her hair, Marcus turned on the game to watch while sitting on the apartment's small couch. Realizing he was outnumbered 2 to 1, Marcus still tried his luck, but he was quickly voted out and sent to his room like a child. Once finished, Chelby abruptly got up and ran into the bathroom to check out her new hairstyle. She loved it, combing her hair bang down over and over. Mia stayed on the couch and switched channels to one of her Sunday shows.

Chelby began to walk back into the living room as her arm with the tree-like tattoo started to itch. At first, it itched just a little, but then the itching progressed. A faint glow bounced off the right side of the wall as she slowly made it into the living room, her arm now throbbing similar to a heartbeat.

"Ma... Ma... Mom! It's happening again!" Chelby said as she grabbed her arm. Just as Mia looked up to respond to Chelby, Chelby gave off a growling scream. "Daddy, it hurts!" she shouted out as she clenched her fist with the comb still in hand. Marcus ran out of the bedroom, and Mia jumped up from the couch.

"Chelby, what's wrong!" Marcus yelled down the hallway.

In a matter of seconds, Chelby began to disappear. First, her socks, followed by her legs. Then her hands, followed by her arms. Her torso followed by her head until she was no longer in sight.

"My GOD!" Mia mumbled, muffled with her hand over her mouth.

"Chelby, Chelby!" Marcus yelled. The comb in Chelby's hands dropped to the floor and was now visible by both Mia and Marcus.

"What in the world? Chelby? Where are you?" Marcus shouted.

"I'm right here, Daddy. You don't see me?" Chelby puzzlingly asked.

"No, baby, I don't see you!" Marcus replied. The itching completely had stopped, along with the pain abruptly leaving Chelby's arm.

She gave a big sigh of relief and once again said, "Daddy, I'm right here!" Just as she said that, she became visible in precisely reverse order of how she disappeared.

Her head and torso reappeared. Then her arms and hands, followed by her legs and socks.

"Baby!" Mia said, running over to hug Chelby. Marcus slowly walked over to Chelby with a puzzled look on his face. While Mia was still hugging her only child in her hands, Marcus leaned over to kiss Chelby on her forehead.

He looked her over up and down and then placed his hand on top of her head while looking up and said, "What is going on...?" Suddenly, Marcus's facial expression changed as if he just figured out the equation of a test. He looked at both Mia and Chelby twice over before blurting out, "It's her hair!"

"Her hair?" Mia curiously asked.

"My hair?" Chelby questioned seconds after her mother spoke. They both looked at Marcus with a puzzling look, trying to figure out what he meant by his statement.

"Chelby, when you pushed the large couch clear down the hall with little to no effort, what were you doing before that?" Marcus asked. Chelby and Mia looked even more puzzled than before, but Marcus continued. "When your mother told me about what happened that day, she started by saying she had just finished doing your hair on the couch. Now today, a few minutes after your hair was done, you started to disappear. There's something to that, Chelby," Marcus concluded.

With Mia finally gathering her thoughts, she spoke. "So, you think her hair is the reason for these abilities, due to the lightning?" Mia asked.

"Yeah, I do. This can't be a coincidence," Marcus replied.

"Daddy might be right, Mom. It sounds strange, but what's happening to me is pretty strange too," Chelby admitted.

"Marcus, you have a point. It's just a lot to take in," Mia responded.

"I don't know exactly how it happened, but you were electrocuted, recovered miraculously fast, and now having these abilities. It seems to all be connected, somehow," Marcus proclaimed.

"Marcus, this feels crazy to say, and I'm not sure if I totally agree; matter of fact, I don't know, never mind," Mia replied.

Chelby quietly stood by and listened as both parents discussed how the tragic events they experienced may have everything to do with the unique abilities Chelby seemed to now possess.

"Chelby, what do you think?" Marcus asked.

"I mean, I do see the connection Dad, but I just don't understand how this is happening," Chelby replied.

"Question, baby, do you remember how you were able to reappear again after disappearing?" Marcus asked. Chelby thought for a second before answering.

"Well, once you said you couldn't see me, I just thought in my head of being seen," Chelby responded.

"Explain, Chelby," Marcus said.

"It's difficult to explain, but I thought about you and Mom seeing me, and that's when y'all were able to see me again."

Marcus put his hand over his mustache, then with one finger, grazed over his lips. He began to mumble something, thinking out loud to himself. "Chelby, see if you can push the big couch down the hall again," Marcus asked of Chelby.

"Marcus?!" Mia questioned sternly.

"Amia, I just want to see something," Marcus explained.

"Ok, Daddy, I'll try," Chelby got behind the heavy couch, took a quick breath, and pushed. The couch barely budged. She took a step back and made an even longer inhale before going with all her might. The couch hardly moved once again. "I don't get it, Dad. You were trying to give me a quick workout or something. I almost sweated out my new hairstyle," Chelby joked. Her mother shook her head with an uncomfortable smile on her face while her father tried to figure out why she couldn't move the couch this time.

"Mia, last time Chelby didn't have this same hairstyle, did she?" Marcus asked.

"No, she didn't, but what does that have to do with anything?" Mia asked. He paused to gather his thoughts before speaking again. "It might have something to do with everything," Marcus responded.

"Last time, she was able to push this heavy couch and that big boy with little to no effort, right?" Marcus asked both Chelby and Mia. They both acknowledged him by nodding their heads as he continued. "All of a sudden, she disappears after getting her hair done this time but is unable to push the couch again, right?" Marcus asked. They both stood there listening and trying to figure out what Marcus was getting at. "It has to be because her hair is different from before," Marcus explained.

"So, wait, Dad, you think every time I get a new hairstyle that I will have a new ability?" Chelby asked.

"Yeah, Chelby, I think so, but not only that, the ability you had prior may be gone!" Marcus responded.

"Wow, that's crazy!" Mia replied.

"Chelby, do me a favor; I want you to try and disappear again, just like before," Marcus asked.

Chelby sighed before responding. "Ok, Dad, I'll try," Chelby replied.

Chelby thought about disappearing again, and at that very moment, just like before, she did. First, her feet and legs were no longer visible. Then her hands and arms, followed by her stomach and head.

"Chelby, enough! Come back!" Mia demanded.

Chelby thought about reappearing after her mother's demands and did just that. Just as fast as she was gone, she came back in clear sight. First, her head and torso, followed by her arms and hands. Lastly, with the reappearance of her legs and feet.

"You see!" Marcus said, with a big smile on his face. "I'm not as crazy as y'all think."

Mia couldn't believe what she saw, and for the second time at that. Chelby sat back down on the couch behind her, more confused than ever before.

"So, what do you think is happening to Chelby, Marcus?" Mia asked.

"I don't know, babe, but it's something special," he responded. It was starting to get late, and once Mia realized how late, she headed into the bathroom to take a quick shower for the night. As Mia was in the bathroom, Marcus and Chelby talked more about these strange but incredible abilities.

"I don't understand why this is happening to me, Daddy. I just don't get it," Chelby said to her father.

"You know something, you are beautiful like your mother, but we share a lot of the same characteristics," Marcus mentioned. "How you love to help people, you have such a great heart," her father reminded her. "Any time we would pass a homeless person in the streets, Chelby, you'd always ask your mother and me to give money to them. You love helping others. You've always been that way," Marcus said with a face full of admiration.

"But I'm not going to be Superman, Dad. You do know that, right?" Chelby asked.

"Of course not, more like Supergirl!" Marcus replied, smiling.

"No, but seriously Dad, all of this is too much," Chelby responded.

Marcus sat down closer to Chelby and hugged her. "I'm gonna tell you a secret, Chelby, that I never told you before," Marcus said. "When you were about three, I had the most vivid dream I've ever had, and you were in it," Marcus said as Chelby looked and listened on. "In my dream, I was falling and scared. Once I finally hit the ground, I looked, and there was a huge tree far in the distance. I walked to this tree, and there were little kids, older kids, black, white, all different colors and nationalities in this giant tree. Once I got closer, I could tell they couldn't get down or out of the tree. As I got even closer, I could hear the cries for help and see the tears running down from some of their faces. When I got close enough, I could see the children's eyes looking down at somebody. It was a woman, and it looked like they were begging for her to save them. Once the woman turned around, it was you!

Just an older and more mature looking you, but it was you, Chelby. You didn't speak, but you smiled at me, and I woke up crying, " Marcus concluded.

"Wow, I can't believe that Dad. What do you think that means?" Chelby curiously asked.

"I always felt there was something special about you, different from the normal feelings a father feels about a child. But after the dream that night, I was sure of it. God meant for you to help people, Chelby," Marcus exclaimed.

"Help people how though, Dad? Isn't that what police officers and firefighters are for?" Chelby questioned.

"Although those you just mentioned are heroes in every sense of the word Chelby, there are always ways people can help," Marcus responded. "These are jobs that are extremely dangerous, and I would never want you to do anything dangerous, especially as a child," he continued. "You see how you took up for that student from being bullied in school; that's what heroes do! Or when you courageously questioned that teacher in his classroom about his conduct with the students, that was heroic as well!" Marcus continued.

Chelby had a nervous smile on her face as she looked on while her father continued speaking. She listened, and when agreeing with him, she nodded her head several times.

"Every hero does not wear a cape and fly around saving cats from trees, Chelby," Marcus said as Chelby giggled. "The real heroes stand up for people that can't stand up for themselves. If they see or hear someone being abused, they help in whatever way they can. They use whatever abilities they possess to do what's right and not ignore those in need. So, the truth is Chelby, you've always been a hero but just didn't know it," Marcus concluded.

"Maybe you're right, Dad!" Chelby replied. Marcus gave Chelby a big hug as she hugged him back. "I want you always to be safe and smart first, and never do anything that can possibly get you hurt, ok?" Marcus told Chelby. "But I do believe God has given you these abilities to help people. We just have to figure out how and to make sure nobody notices," Marcus said.

Chelby stayed quiet for a second as thoughts ran through her head. Her facial expression looked very similar to her father's when figuring something out or coming up with an idea. "Hey, Dad, do you still have that small camcorder you took with us on vacation a couple of years ago?" Chelby asked.

"Camcorder, for what?" Mia asked. As she was finishing in the bathroom, she overheard some of the conversation walking back into the living room. With both Mia and Marcus waiting for a response, Chelby responded.

"Mom, Dad...I have an idea," Chelby replied.

Chapter 4

C-Mac

"An idea about what Chelby?" her mother asked.

"Yeah, baby, what's on your mind?" her father added.

"Well, Dad, remember what we were just talking about, right? I think I have an idea of how I can help the students that are possibly being mistreated at my school by Mr. McIntosh," Chelby replied.

Mia looked slightly confused as Marcus looked on, eager to hear Chelby's idea. Both parents waited as their not-so-little girl spoke on the thoughts of her plans. Chelby explained how her fresh, new ability could catch Mr. McIntosh with his disgusting behavior towards the young students.

"But how, Chelby?" Mia questioned. Chelby explained with the camcorder; she would stand somewhere in the classroom to record Mr. McIntosh's actions without being seen.

"What about the camcorder, Chelby? It'll be floating in midair like a ghost," Mia asked.

Chelby smiled before responding, "No, Mom, just like the comb, it'll disappear in my hand once I do, remember?" Marcus smirked before saying what was on his mind. "It actually sounds like a good plan, Chelby, but I don't want you to get hurt or find yourself in trouble of any kind," Marcus explained. "As I told you earlier tonight, your safety and well-being mean everything to me," Marcus continued.

"I know it does, Dad, but I'll be fine," Chelby replied. "Like we also discussed, I have to try to help those unable to help themselves," Chelby added.

"She's right, Mia, that is what I told her," Marcus responded. "Wait, wait, wait, are y'all both crazy or something? Listen, Marcus, I agree with that as well. I just worry about the trouble this can cause in and out of school. That's my biggest concern," Mia responded.

"Mom, I promise I'll be ok," Chelby replied.

"Chelby, you can't promise that. You don't know what's going to happen if you try to go through with this crazy plan of yours," Mia replied.

"Mom, trust me, if I feel like something is going wrong, I will make sure to get out of there before anyone notices me, I promise," Chelby responded.

Mia reluctantly nodded as Marcus went to his room to find the camcorder to give to Chelby. After rumbling through his closet, he found it and brought it out.

"Listen, girl, make sure this camera comes back in one piece, or you gonna disappear for real!" Marcus jokingly demanded.

Mia slowly shook her head back and forth. "Ok, Chelby, get ready for bed. School is tomorrow," Mia instructed.

"Ok, Mom, have a goodnight. Love you," Chelby replied, heading into the bathroom. Her father wished her goodnight before returning to the couch to finish watching TV. The following day Chelby woke up anxious but ready to go through with her plan. She packed her father's small camcorder in her bag, along with her books and other items for school.

"Can't believe you are going to go through with this, Chelby. You're a brave little girl, but I must be crazy for allowing this," Mia acknowledged.

"Yeah, I know, Mom, but I have to. This is something I just have to do," Chelby replied.

Once reaching school, Chelby had to figure out how she would leave her class and sneak into Mr. Mcintosh's class without being noticed. She thought she should ask Shyla for some help during lunch.

"Hey Shyla, I need a favor that could possibly get you in trouble," Chelby said.

"I'm down. What is it?" Shyla replied. "Ok, well, I have to sneak off to another class for a few minutes, and I need you to cover for me until I get back," Chelby explained.

"Ok, cool, but you owe me an extra ice cream sandwich when Ms. Kaylie comes by today, deal?" Shyla replied.

"Ms. Kaylie, who is that?" Chelby asked.

"You don't know Ms. Kaylie, the ice cream truck lady? Last weekend when it was kind of warm out, she came around, so I'm hoping she comes back around today since it's warm again," Shyla explained.

"Oh, ok, I haven't seen her yet, but a woman ice cream lady, that's pretty cool," Chelby replied.

"She's really cool and sweet too. Sometimes she even gives us extra ice cream without paying," Shyla mentioned.

"Wow, that is pretty cool, but yeah, I got you later if she comes around," Chelby replied.

"So, what time are you going?" Shyla asked.

"I'll probably go during gym, so if the gym teacher asks, just tell him I'm in the bathroom not feeling well," Chelby replied.

"Ok, cool, no problem," Shyla responded.

Before lunch was over, Chelby headed up to Mr. Mcintosh's classroom. She stood two doors down to ensure that neither Mr. McIntosh nor the kids were in yet. Soon as she knew it was safe to go, she hurried right in.

She thought about hiding in the closet or by the window but eventually picked a corner in the back of the class. She had to focus, and quickly, she thought, before Mr. McIntosh and the students rushed in. "Disappear! Disappear!" she whispered to herself. But it didn't work. She took a deep breath to calm down and refocus, and that's when it happened. Her arm began to itch as her shoes and legs began to vanish before her eyes. Then her arms and hands, followed by her torso and head. She stood in the back as the young students came into the classroom. She saw young Cameron and caught herself about to say hi as he walked in.

"Ok, everybody, take a seat. Lunch is over!" Mr. McIntosh shouted as he closed the classroom door. The kids sat down as their smiles and laughter quickly turned into joyless quietness. Chelby stood unseen in the corner, trying her best not to breathe loud, but was ready to record everything.

"Ok, guys, it's time for your math quiz, and I only want pencils and papers out!" Mr. McIntosh demanded as he walked around the classroom. He counted down from five to one before heading back up to the front of the class to give the test. "Nicole Brown, is that a folder there still on your desk after I gave the countdown?" Mr. McIntosh asked sternly. The little girl frantically put the folder back in her bag with a worrisome look on her face. "You must be both deaf and dumb; get up and stand in the back facing the wall until the test is over," Mr. McIntosh snarled. Mr. McIntosh looked around the class for more disobedience.

"Randy!" he screamed as he walked over to him. Something caught Mr. Mcintosh's eye. Randy still had his math worksheet sticking out of his bag. Mr. McIntosh pinched him on his arm while pointing to the paper before screaming in his face. "Are you crazy? Were you about to cheat on my test, boy?!" The frightened student shook his head no, but Mr. McIntosh refused to believe him. "Get your lying self to the back of the class with the other one, and don't you dare turn around till I say," Mr. McIntosh demanded. "Can't ever trust you, people," Mr. McIntosh added.

You people? Chelby thought to herself.

"I don't know what's wrong with you students. You all refuse to listen. You'll never make it in this world, just a bunch of losers taking up space!" Mr. McIntosh concluded.

Chelby stood there, recording everything unnoticed by anybody else in the room. She felt angry that the young students had to go through this but overjoyed she could catch everything on camera.

Once the quiz was over, Mr. Mcintosh told the students standing to sit back down in their assigned seats. Afterward, Mr. McIntosh went to the back of the classroom to go into his supply closet. He brought out work to start the lesson he had planned for the remainder of the day. As he was doing this, Chelby slowly walked to the front of the class and cracked open the door, just enough for her to slide out.

After she was able to leave out of the classroom successfully, and as she hurried off to gym class, Chelby overheard Mr. McIntosh asking about the cracked opened door as she left. Chelby ran into the bathroom before entering the gym to change back to normal.

Back to her normal state, Chelby went to the gym teacher to tell him that she was feeling better. She didn't want to lie but thought it was for the better good, this time.

Once school ended, Chelby had to keep her promise to Shyla and get her those ice cream sandwiches she agreed to get. "Yes, here comes Ms. Kaylie now. Told you!" Shyla said. Chelby never met anybody who got so excited over food.

"Oh yeah, I see her," Chelby admitted. Once the truck stopped, all the other kids got in line, along with Shyla.

"Hey kids, what can I get y'all," Ms. Kaylie asked. The kids shouted out different orders as Ms. Kaylie got them all what they wanted individually. She was an older woman with a friendly smile and short haircut that Chelby noticed right away. After Shyla received what she asked for, she introduced Chelby to Ms. Kaylie.

"Hey, Ms. Kaylie, this is my friend Chelby," Shyla mentioned.

"Oh, so nice to meet you, Chelby, you're such a beautiful girl, and I just love your hair," Ms. Kaylie replied.

"Thank you, Ms. Kaylie. Nice to meet you as well," Chelby responded.

"Two beautiful girls, that are friends too? Watch out, world!" Ms. Kaylie said before driving off. The kids waved to her as she drove away.

"Told you Ms. Kaylie was nice," Shyla said.

"Yeah, she is. You were right," Chelby agreed.

Chelby couldn't wait to get home to show her parents what she recorded at school. When her father got home, they all watched what was on the camcorder. Chelby's parents were disgusted at what they saw. Marcus told Mia to go up to school with Chelby along with the footage to bring it to the principal the very next day.

As they all were discussing the footage, something came on the news that caught their attention. It was news about a young girl that's been missing for two weeks now. She lived not too far from where Chelby and her parents lived, which drew even more attention to the TV.

"Theirs a lot of crazy people out there, Chelby, that's why we constantly worry about you," Marcus declared.

"I just know her parents are going nuts without her right now. See, even though we can be annoying at times, we only do it for your safety," Mia replied.

"I know, Mom, I know. I feel sad for both the little girl and her parents," Chelby replied.

"Let's just hope the cops can find her and bring her back home to her parents safely and soon," Marcus mentioned.

The next morning, Mia went up to school with Chelby to show the principal what Chelby had recorded.

Since it was such a busy morning this particular day, Chelby and Mia were asked to sit and wait to speak with the principal by a clerk in the office. Chelby thought most mornings must have been highly active for the principal because she barely had seen him face to face. Luckily Ms. Bell, the assistant principal, abruptly walked in not too long after Mia and Chelby were asked to sit and wait.

"Hey, Ms. Bell, how are you?" Mia asked, getting Ms. Bell's attention.

"Oh, hey Mrs. Williams, how are you? Something I can help you with?" Ms. Bell asked as she scattered about the room.

"Actually, you can, Ms. Bell, but it's extremely private. Do you mind if we go into your office to talk?" Chelby's mother requested.

"Um, sure, give me one second, though, please," Ms. Bell replied. Ms. Bell busily moved around the office for the next few minutes, taking care of what she needed to as Mia and Chelby waited for her. "Mrs. Williams, you and Chelby can come in now," Ms. Bell said as she held the door open for Chelby and Mia to enter her office.

"Sorry about the wait, but some mornings can be hectic around here," Ms. Bell explained.

"It's ok, I understand, and thank you for giving us your time," Mia replied.

"So, ladies, what can I help y'all with today," Ms. Bell asked. Mia motioned and pointed to the bag Chelby was carrying.

"Show her, Chelby," Mia requested. Chelby took the camcorder out of her bookbag before explaining.

"Ok, Ms. Bell, this is going to sound weird, but it's true," Chelby admitted.

"Well, try me, what's wrong?" Ms. Bell asked.

"Well, on my very first day of school, I witnessed Mr. McIntosh react extremely rude to his students," Chelby said as Ms. Bell listened and looked on. "Then, you know the program after school that allows older students to tutor and mentor younger students, right?" Chelby asked.

"Yes, I do," Ms. Bell responded.

"Well, I tutor one of the students in Mr. Mcintosh's class, who told me that he also pinches them and screams at them when they do something that he doesn't like," Chelby added.

"What? Mr. McIntosh? Which student is this?" Ms. Bell asked. "I'd rather not say, but I believed this student 100 percent!" Chelby replied.

"I know Mr. McIntosh has his ways, but this is all new to me. He's been teaching for so long, so it's hard to believe this hasn't come up before," Ms. Bell responded.

"From what the student told me, Ms. Bell, when he finds something unacceptable, he scares the students into not telling what really happens in his class when you don't do as he says."

"Wow, Chelby, these are some serious accusations you are saying right now. You do understand that, right?" Ms. Bell said.

"Yes, I do, Ms. Bell," Chelby replied.

"To be honest with you, Chelby, sometimes younger children have a great imagination and tend to lie at times, as well," Ms. Bell responded.

"Yes, I know and agree with that, Ms. Bell, but not this time," Chelby replied. Chelby stood up and walked to Ms. Bell's desk to show her what she recorded. "Press play, Ms. Bell, please," Chelby requested.

Ms. Bell pressed play and began to look on with Chelby. As the recording played, Ms. Bell's facial expression changed several times. From puzzled, to a shocking look, to lastly, an angry and concerning look. Ms. Bell viewed all she needed to see.

"I can't believe this. How did you even get this recording?" Ms. Bell eagerly asked. Chelby and Mia looked at one another before Chelby answered.

"Well, to be honest, I snuck into Mr. Mcintosh's class and recorded while standing in the corner of the room," Chelby replied.

"Did you, huh, and no one saw you?" Ms. Bell asked.

"No, I don't think so. Guess it was a great hiding spot," Chelby said as she nervously grinned. Mia smirked at Chelby's last statement as well.

"Well, I guess it was," Ms. Bell chuckled.

"I'm going to have to hold onto what you just presented to me, ladies, as actions may need to be taken for Mr. Mcintosh's lack of professionalism," Ms. Bell explained. Both Mia and Chelby nodded their heads in agreement.

"You were one brave little girl to hide in Mr. Mcintosh's room to record this footage like that. I applaud you, Chelby. I know it must have been scary, but a brave and noble act indeed," Ms. Bell said.

"Thank you, Ms. Bell. I just wanted the younger students to be unafraid while in school. School shouldn't be a place of fear," Chelby replied.

Both Ms. Bell and Mia smiled after Chelby made her last statement. "You're absolutely right, Chelby, and you did a great thing," Ms. Bell mentioned.

"Um, Ms. Bell, can you not mention the fact that I recorded this to Mr. McIntosh, please? I don't want any trouble," Chelby asked.

"I promise I won't mention your name, but I do have to state that a student recorded this. Don't worry, Chelby. Everything will turn out fine," Ms. Bell concluded.

Ms. Bell shook Mia's hand as both she and Chelby left the office. "Hey, Mom, what do you think is going to happen to Mr. McIntosh? I just wanted him to stop mistreating his students. Do you think he'll be fired?" Chelby asked.

"Truly, I don't know, baby, but that's not up to us now. You did your part. Now we just have to wait and see where things go from here, but just know I'm very proud of you, Chelby. Helping those that are unable to help themselves is a brave and noble thing," Mia looked at Chelby. "Just don't ever do this again! Thank you!" Mia added. Mia kissed Chelby on the forehead and hugged her as she left the school.

Later on, that week, when Chelby saw Cameron at the library for tutoring, she was eager to see what happened with Mr. McIntosh.

"Hey Cameron, how are you?" Chelby asked, waving to Cameron.

"Hey Chelby, I'm good," Cameron replied. Cameron opened up his book, ready to go over his work as usual, because whenever he and Chelby would meet up, they'd do so.

"So how is everything? How has class been, Cameron?" Chelby asked. Chelby hesitated to ask about Mr. McIntosh, hoping Cameron would mention him before she did directly.

"Class has been pretty great, um, you know we have a new teacher now, right? " Cameron asked.

"A new teacher? No, I didn't know," Chelby replied.

"Yes, it's a woman substitute. She said she'd be here for the rest of the month," Cameron responded.

"Wow, so how do you like her so far?" Chelby asked. Cameron gave a big smile before answering.

"She's nice, so far!" Cameron excitedly replied. "Better than Mr. McIntosh," He whispered.

"Well, that's good. I'm just glad you are happy with the new teacher Cameron," Chelby replied.

"Yes, I am. Thank you, Chelby," Cameron said.

"You're very welcome, of course, now let's get to this work!" Chelby responded.

Cameron finished up his work as Chelby looked on. The next day Chelby was curious about what happened to Mr. McIntosh and wondered if he was fired. Chelby was nervous to ask Ms. Bell what happened, but her curiosity led her to Ms. Bell's office anyhow. The office wasn't as crowded as two mornings ago.

"Um, is Ms. Bell busy right now? If not, may I speak with her, please?" Chelby asked the woman in the principal's office.

"Let me go check for you sweety, what's your name?" the woman asked.

"Oh, I'm Chelby Williams," Chelby replied. The woman went into Ms. Bells' office and quickly came back out. Motioning to Chelby to go in, Chelby hustled and nervously walked in.

"Afternoon Ms. Bell, how are you? Chelby asked.

"Afternoon to you, Ms. Chelby, I'm doing just fine, and yourself?" Ms. Bell responded.

"Um, I'm doing good, thank you," Chelby responded nervously. "Sorry to bother you, but I have a question to ask."

"Oh, you're no bother honey, what's the question?" Ms. Bell asked.

"Well, I was wondering what happened with Mr. McIntosh? Remember the young student I tutor from the program? I was told that Mr. McIntosh wasn't teaching his class anymore," Chelby said. Chelby was very careful not to mention Cameron's name in hopes of not getting him involved.

"Well, Chelby, that student you tutor is right. He is not teaching here at the moment," Ms. Bell responded.

"Oh no, was he fired?" Chelby asked.

"Well, I'm not supposed to speak of this matter nor the outcome of it with students, but no, he wasn't terminated. Right now, he is on a 30-day suspension upon further review," Ms. Bell added.

"Oh wow, well, I'm glad he's not fired, at least," Chelby replied.

"Yes, he's just suspended for now, but this is what happens when you do the wrong thing. That's why you must always try your best to do the right thing, even when it's tough to do. Never forget that." Ms. Bell placed a reassuring hand on Chelby's shoulder. "With that said, Chelby, here you did the right thing, and I hope you continue to be that way as you get older," Ms. Bell concluded.

"I will, Ms. Bell, I will, and thank you for your time. Have a nice day!" Chelby replied as she began to walk out of the office.

"You have a great day as well honey. Say hello to your mother for me," Ms. Bell responded.

"I will!" Chelby answered as she left the office. Later on that day, after school, Shyla asked for Chelby to wait with her for a few minutes while she waited for her mother to pick her up for dance practice. "Your mother is a little late today, huh?" Chelby asked.

"Yeah, she's always a little late," Shyla admitted.

"So, what's good with your mom's shop? I thought it'd be up and running by now?" Shyla asked.

"Yeah, I know, my mother did too. Guess it's taking longer than we expected," Chelby responded. That's cool, as long as it's fine by summertime, I'm good," Shyla replied.

"Oh yeah, it'll be fine by then for sure," Chelby said.

"Oh yeah, don't forget to ask your mother if you can come to the winter show next Friday," Shyla mentioned.

"Oh, that's right, and you're in the show too, right, Shyla?" Chelby asked. "Yup, I already have my dress, just gotta figure out how I should do my hair," Shyla replied.

"Oh, that's so cool. I almost forgot. I noticed the flyer on the wall the other day with your name on the list of students performing in the show. Glad you reminded me," Chelby responded.

"It's going to be cool after the show too. It's going to be a dance for the 5th and 6th graders in the gym directly after," Shyla said.

"That's right. I did see that, too. That should be nice," Chelby replied.

They continued to discuss back and forth about the show and school dance. As they continued their conservation in front of the school, down the block from where Chelby and Shyla stood, they noticed the ice cream truck slowly approaching.

"Chelby, look! Yes, it's Ms. Kaylie!" Shyla said, licking her lips.

I can't believe Ms. Kaylie came around today, Chelby thought. "First off, it's way too cold for ice cream today; and second, don't you have dance practice in a few minutes?" Chelby asked.

"First, it's never too cold for ice cream, and second, since it is cold, I can leave it in my bag for later, duh!" Shyla responded, smiling.

Ms. Kaylie slowly approached the girls and the small number of kids that happened to be hanging outside of school. "Hey, Ms. Kaylie! Hi, Ms. Kaylie," students outside the school said, waving.

"Hey guys, what would you like today?" Ms. Kaylie asked. All the kids had smiles on their faces, which Chelby thought was so weird.

"Hey girls, would you like something?" Ms. Kaylie asked Chelby and Shyla.

"Well, of course, she does, Ms. Kaylie, but I'm good, thank you," Chelby responded.

"Ok, no problem, dear. It's Chelby, right?" Ms. Kaylie asked.

"Yes, it is, " Chelby replied.

"So, my pretty little Shyla, you want the regular, right, ice cream sandwiches?" Ms. Kaylie asked.

"Oh, how you know me so well, Ms. Kaylie. Yes, please!" Shyla eagerly responded.

Ms. Kaylie gave all the students what they asked for and even threw in an extra treat or two to be nice. Not too long after Ms. Kaylie left, Ms. Baxter's car drove up to pick up Shyla for practice. The two girls said their goodbyes, and afterward, Chelby headed home.

Chapter 5

Ms. Kaylie's Secret

That weekend the Williams family decided to go bowling. After a great afternoon family outing, they headed home to relax before Sunday's dinner. Marcus went straight to his room for his usual Sunday nap as Mia started cooking and Chelby watched TV. Chelby told her mother about the little meeting she and Ms. Bell had concerning Mr. McIntosh. Mia admitted that she was eager to find out about the punishment, if any, that would be handed down to him by the school.

Some time passed while Mia prepared the food. Although hungry, Chelby's eyes focused on the TV screen in front of her. As she was flipping through channels, it happened to end up on the local news.

"Hey, Mom, look!" Chelby exclaimed. She brought Mia's attention to the TV, in which the report was about the young girl that went missing a couple of weeks back. The picture on the screen was of a 6-year-old girl, fair-skinned, with short dark brown hair.

"Wow, they still haven't found that little girl? Unbelievable," Mia murmured.

At that moment, Marcus was walking from his room into the living room.

"Sad, right, Mia? That's why I hardly ever watch the news. It stays with negativity," Marcus mentioned. Marcus had woke up from his nap and was watching the news as well from his room. "You probably don't remember this, Chelby, but you and I had a code to prevent a tragedy like this from happening to you," Marcus added.

Chelby and Mia looked at one another as if Marcus was crazy. "Marcus, go back to sleep. You must still be tired talking about some code mess," Mia replied. Chelby laughed out loud, thinking the same thing.

"I know, I know, I'm the crazy one. Well, watch this, Mia; let's see if she remembers," Marcus replied. "Hey Chelby, what's the word?" Chelby looked confused as Marcus repeated himself. "Chelby, what's the word?" Marcus demanded.

Chelby looked confused but then answered. "Thun-der-bird…?"

Marcus smiled, glancing over to Mia. "And what's the price?" Marcus asked.

"Mighty nice!" Chelby replied. Marcus pulled Chelby in for a hug then gave her a two-hand-five.

"You see Mia, she remembered!" Marcus shouted.

"Wait, where is that from again?" Mia questioned.

"I taught Chelby that rhyme when she was little. So, just in case anybody told Chelby that we said for her to go with them, but we didn't," Marcus explained. "If they didn't know that code, for Chelby to run away to safety screaming if she had to until we got to her," Marcus added.

"Wow, Dad, I do remember now," Chelby admitted.

"I knew you would, baby. The reason why I brought that up was because of the news we just saw. A quick riddle like that, taught and instilled in a young child, just might prevent something tragic like this from happening to them," Marcus explained.

"You're right, Marcus; I remember it now, too," Mia admitted. "Your mother doesn't remember," Marcus whispered to Chelby as they both tried to hide their laughter.

"What was that!?" Mia demanded.

"Oh nothing, babe, dinner smells great, though. Is it almost ready?" Marcus asked.

"Yeah, whatever, but yes, it is," Mia replied.

After enjoying their dinner, the three of them headed to the living room to relax. Chelby almost forgot to mention to her parents about Shyla's show and to ask them if she could attend the dance directly after. "Hey Mom, Dad, I wanted to ask y'all something," Chelby said.

"What is it, baby?" Marcus asked as he got up to wash the dishes.

"I wanted to know if I could go to the winter show that Shyla is performing in at school this Saturday?" Chelby asked. "Oh, that shouldn't be a problem at all," Mia replied.

"They are also having a dance for the 5th and 6th graders right after. You think I can go to that too?" Chelby added.

"A dance..., with boys?!" Marcus asked.

"Of course, with boys, you know she has boys at her school, right?" Mia budded in to mention. Marcus' eyebrows went up as he frowned. "Don't pay him any mind, Chelby. What time are the show and dance starting and ending?" Mia asked.

"Well, I think the show starts from 2 pm to 4 pm, and the dance is from 4 pm to 6 pm directly after," Chelby replied.

Marcus stood quietly, listening with the same expression on his face. "Hey, Dad, it's supposed to be warmer on Saturday. Do you think I can get a new dress for the show and dance?" Chelby asked.

"Oh, so now it's hey Dad, before it was, pay him no mind. So let me get this straight, you want a new dress, and there's going to be boys there?!" Marcus questioned, raising his voice.

"Listen, we'll go to the mall early on Saturday and see if we can find you something nice but not too expensive. If we can't, you'll just have to wear something nice that you already have. Ok, Chelby?" Mia concluded. Marcus threw up his hands while shaking his head and walked out of the room.

"Ok, thanks, Mom. Do you think Daddy is really upset?" Chelby asked.

"No, no, he's being dramatic. He'll be just fine," Mia responded. "So, what hairstyle do you think I should get today since I've had this one for two weeks now? I kinda wanted something new," Chelby explained.

"Oh, for a dance, I think you should have your hair up," Mia replied.

"Oh yeah, that sounds cool, like in a bun?" Chelby asked.

"Exactly, it's called a braided updo bun. I think you'll love it!" Mia responded.

"Oh man, you're right. I think so too," Chelby replied.

"Yes, with some cute earrings and that necklace your father bought you, you'll look beautiful!" Mia added.

"Ok, Mom, let's do it!" Chelby agreed.

Marcus walked back out to the kitchen to get some juice, poured it, and with a glass in hand, walked right back to his room. "Just to let y'all both know, I ain't paying for jack!" Marcus shouted, poking his head out of his room.

Chelby and Mia busted out laughing. "Hey baby, go get the stuff so we can do your hair. I'll be waiting for you on the couch," Mia said.

"Ok, Mom," Chelby replied as she headed into the bathroom to get what was needed. Chelby hustled back out to the living room, and the two sat down in their usual spots making sure they were both able to watch TV. They were so into the show neither of them realized how fast Mia finished Chelby's hair this time.

"I'm done, Chelby, go take a look," Mia said. Chelby took a second to get a drink and headed to the bathroom to look. "Chelby, wait, come here. How do you feel?" Mia asked.

"Oh, I feel great, Mom, thanks," Chelby replied. At that moment, with Chelby's main focus being on her hair, she didn't realize her mother's concerns and worries over what may happen next.

Chelby walked into the bathroom and looked over her hair from different positions and angles. "Hey, Mom, this style looks so pretty on me," Chelby mentioned. Chelby walked into her parent's bedroom to get the handheld mirror on her mother's dresser to see the back of her hair entirely. "Daddy, what do you think?" Chelby asked.

"Oh, it looks beautiful baby, your mother did a great job as usual," Marcus replied. Soon after her father's response, Chelby's arm began to itch some.

"Baby, you ok?" Marcus asked.

"Yes, I'm good, Dad," Chelby responded. But Chelby's arm began to itch more and more, forcing her to scratch continuously.

"Chelby?!" Marcus shouted. Chelby gave out a slight growl, then yelled and crouched over her parent's bed. Marcus jumped up out of bed to hold Chelby as she tried to catch her breath. Mia came running into the bedroom to see if Chelby was ok.

"Chelby?!" Mia screamed while running to her. Chelby slowly stood up as she began to feel like herself again.

"I'm ok, Mom, you see, I'm good," Chelby assured. Mia took Chelby from Marcus and held her in her arms. She let her embrace go for a second to look Chelby over from head to toe before quickly hugging her again. *Thank God, no crazy abilities this time. Thank goodness for that,* Mia thought.

"Yeah, Mom, no crazy abilities this time. You worry too much," Chelby said.

"Huh?" Mia responded.

"Yeah, Mom, I'm saying, I'm good...no crazy abilities this time," Chelby repeated.

"Baby, I didn't say anything," Mia responded.

"Mom, what are you talking about? I heard what you just said," Chelby replied. Mia took a step back from her daughter to explain.

"Chelby, I didn't say anything... but that was...what I was thinking," Mia admitted.

Chelby looked at her father with a puzzling look, hoping that maybe he could make her understand what exactly her mother was trying to say.

"Um, yeah, baby, I-I was standing right here; your mother didn't say a word," Marcus said.

"So, wait, are you saying that I was able to hear your thoughts?" Chelby asked. Both Mia and Marcus turned to one another, unsure of how to answer. Chelby turned to look at her father as he rubbed his forehead, taking a deep inhale before slowly releasing the air out, letting out a big sigh. Marcus then reached out and grabbed Chelby's hand firmly.

"Miracle, how is this some kind of miracle? I don't want to be able to read anyone's thoughts," Chelby shouted.

"Chelby, I didn't say anything, but I was thinking that just now. Wow," Marcus murmured.

"Oh, my goodness! Now I have to hear people's thoughts all day long. This thing is the worst!" Chelby shouted. Chelby stormed out of the room as her parent's followed behind her.

"Wait, baby, wait, calm down, please," Marcus demanded.

"Calm down? Daddy, you think this is cool?" Chelby asked, turning around to face her father.

"You thought the sudden strength you had was crazy or that your ability to disappear was weird, but those abilities both were beneficial to others. Chelby, you see, sometimes just being normal is not good enough. Like I explained to you before, special people use their gifts, whatever they may be, to help those who are unable to help themselves," Marcus concluded.

"As crazy as whatever is happening to you is, your father has a point," Mia replied.

"Ok, but, Mom, hearing people's thoughts other than my own all day is going to drive me crazy," Chelby admitted.

"Well, maybe not, Chelby, if you learn how to control it somehow," Marcus replied.

"Ok, Dad, but how, this is so frustrating," Chelby responded, rolling her eyes. "

"Well, let's try to figure it out together. You haven't read our minds as we were talking just now; maybe we have to be silent," Marcus suggested.

"So, let's be quiet for a second then, and let's see what happens," Mia added. The three of them stood still and quiet in the living room waiting, but as moments passed, Chelby could read neither her mother nor her father's thoughts at that time.

"Ok, so that didn't work," Mia blurted out.

"We have to think what Chelby was doing as she read our minds," Marcus added. They took a second trying to figure out how this new ability worked.

"Well, Dad, I was looking at you and Mom at the time y'all say I read your mind, so maybe that's how," Chelby mentioned. Marcus listened and walked to Chelby, now face to face with her, to see if it worked, but it didn't. Marcus then playfully grabbed both of Chelby's arms as she did it back to him, shaking her, attempting to shake the ability to work.

Man, nothing, this ability is weird for real, Marcus thought.

"Told you, Dad, this thing was weird!" Chelby blurted out.

Marcus looked at Chelby with a smile and said, "I didn't say a word, baby, not one word," Marcus replied. "You must be able to read minds when you touch someone," Marcus stated.

"Oh, you might be right, Dad. Let me try it on, Mom," Chelby responded.

Chelby walked over to her mother to see if what her father said was true.

"So, Mia, don't say anything, but think something," Marcus requested. Chelby put her arm around her mother's waist to half-hug her while Mia stared at Marcus with doubt, who was awaiting any kind of response from either one of them. A few seconds had passed before Chelby took her arm away from her mother's waist.

"Guess that's not it babe. You were wrong this time," Mia said to Marcus. Marcus shook his head with a confused look on his face.

"No way, Mom! It's Daddy's day to wash the dishes!" Chelby exclaimed.

"Huh, what are you talking about, Chelby?" Marcus asked. Chelby smirked as Mia looked back at her in awe.

"Wow, she did it, Marcus. That's what I was thinking," Mia explained. Mia's thoughts were that Chelby should wash the dishes tonight instead of her father.

"Don't worry, Mom, I won't tell Daddy about what else you were thinking," Chelby said before laughing.

"Oh, is that right?" Marcus asked.

"Girl, I'm going to get you!" Mia responded, laughing as well.

"So, listen, tomorrow at school, you're going to have to be extremely careful of who you come in contact with. We don't want anyone noticing this thing," Marcus instructed.

"Yes, Dad, I know," Chelby replied.

"Ok, baby, go get ready for bed. It's been quite a long night, school tomorrow," Mia reminded.

As Chelby hugged them both goodnight, she said, "Yeah, I love y'all too!" Marcus and Mia shook their heads as Chelby headed to the bathroom. "Goodnight, guys!" Chelby added, closing the bathroom door.

"Goodnight baby, goodnight sweetie," both Marcus and Mia replied.

The following day on her way to school, Chelby was nervous about accidentally reading her classmate's minds. *What am I going to do at lunch or gym? This is going to be a rough week*, she thought. As her mother dropped her off in front of the building, Chelby felt almost as nervous as she did on her first day. She paused and took a breath, waved goodbye to her mother, and walked into school. As she walked in, she saw some friends that waved hello to her as they continued to class.

That was cool, she thought. She didn't have to touch anyone, which would ultimately force her to read their minds. Even teachers walked by without touching her, they would say good morning as well, but contact was the only thing that worried Chelby.

Just then, Chelby felt a tug at her hood, then two small hands covering her eyes from behind. It was Shyla. "Hey, Chelby!" Shyla said excitedly.

Shyla came around to hug Chelby as Chelby hugged her back. *This zip-up hood is hot! I wonder where she got it?* Shyla thought.

"Oh, my father bought this for me after my other hood was burnt in the salon," Chelby mentioned.

A confused expression came across Shyla's face as she looked up towards Chelby, puzzled by Chelby's comment. "Huh, what are you talking about, girl?" Shyla asked.

"My hood, you mentioned my hood, right? I was just telling you where I got it from," Chelby responded.

"Girl, I didn't say that, but um, I definitely was thinking that," Shyla admitted. Chelby's face became flush. She was embarrassed she didn't realize she was reading Shyla's thoughts once they embraced.

"Oh right, I knew you were going to say that, though. I know how you are with new clothes, Shyla," Chelby replied. "That's right, girl, you know I'm on it!" Shyla responded.

Whew, that was a close one, Chelby thought. *I have to be much more aware any time I make contact with someone.*

"So, are you ready for your Broadway show?" Chelby asked.

"It's not no Broadway show, Chelby, but yes, I am," Shyla responded, laughing.

Both Chelby and Shyla began to walk towards their classroom as they continued to talk. "Did you remember to ask your parents if you could come to the dance afterward?" Shyla asked.

"Yeah, I did. I almost didn't remember," Chelby replied.

"So, what did they say?" Shyla asked.

"They both said yes, but my mother seemed much more excited about it than my father," Chelby admitted. "That's only cause boys will be there. That's just how fathers are, " Shyla replied.

"Yeah, I guess. My father seemed a little annoyed at first but was fine about it after a while," Chelby responded.

"So, do you know what you're wearing? I'm supposed to get a dress this week sometime after school." Shyla asked.

"Oh, that's cool. I'm not sure yet, but my mother and I are going early on Saturday to see if we can hurry and find something," Chelby replied.

"Oh, that's cool. Just please don't miss any of the show, "Shyla pleaded.

"No way, I definitely won't!" Chelby assured.

With all the talking that Chelby and Shyla were doing back and forth, neither realized that they were right in front of their class now. After walking in, they hung up their coats and other belongings and agreed to finish the conversation later.

That night once both Chelby and Mia settled in, Chelby told her mother about reading Shyla's thoughts accidentally. Mia found it nervously amusing and told

Chelby that she was lucky Shyla wasn't thinking anything wrong about her.

"Just be careful, Chelby, and try to be more observant when you're around your friends," Mia instructed. Chelby agreed with her mother before heading to bed for the night.

The next day after school, she met up with Cameron in his usual spot. Cameron was waiting for Chelby to walk in. As soon as he picked his head up and saw Chelby, he got up and ran to her with a big smile on his face, then hugged her. *I can't wait to tell Chelby about the spelling test*, he excitedly thought.

Chelby smiled. "Wow, Cameron, what's the big hug for? Why are you so happy today?" Chelby asked.

"I got a 100 on the spelling test today Chelby, the first time all year!" Cameron exclaimed.

"What? That's so great, Cameron. I knew you could do it!" Chelby responded. Cameron embarrassingly looked down but then up at Chelby. "What is it Cameron, what's wrong?" Chelby asked.

"Nothing Chelby, just thank you so much for believing in me. That's all," Cameron shyly said. Chelby pulled Cameron in close for another hug.

Chelby is the best, Cameron thought.

"Awe, you're very welcome, Cameron, but thank you for working so hard at something I know you were having trouble with. Like I told you before, practice makes perfect, and always believe in yourself!" Chelby replied.

"You were right, Chelby, thank you, but now let's get to work!" Cameron joked.

"Oh, look at the new Spelling Bee champ go. Ok, Cameron, let's get to work," Chelby responded, smiling.

The rest of the week went pretty smoothly. No one noticed Chelby's abilities. Besides her parents and at times with Shyla, they weren't used very much at all, either. Chelby was looking forward to both the school show and dance. Saturday morning, Chelby and her mother went to check on the salon before heading to the mall. The salon was finally up and running and back to normal as if the tragic events had never occurred. All of Mia's loyal customers were back and even brought some new customers along with them. Everyone was happy that the salon was finally ready and open for business, especially Mia.

After leaving the shop, they rushed to the mall to see if they could find something Chelby would like.

They found a blue lace and flare dress and bought a white sweater top to go over it. Once Mia paid for the dress, the two hurried home to get Chelby ready for the show and dance. Chelby reminded her mother about wearing the necklace her father had bought her, making sure they didn't leave the apartment without it.

After Chelby was fully dressed, Mia rushed her to the school to drop Chelby off. Mia was unable to stay for the show because she had to get back to the salon. Shyla's mother, Ms. Baxter, spoke with Mia earlier that day to inform her not to worry that she, in turn, would stay for the show. So, Ms. Baxter and Shyla awaited for Chelby and her mother to arrive at the school.

When they arrived at the school, Mia said her hellos to both Shyla and her mother as they greeted one another. She abruptly got ready to leave but wished Shyla good luck before she left for the salon. As they were heading into the school, you could hear several kids say, *"Hey, it's Ms. Kaylie!"*

Chelby, Shyla, and Ms. Baxter turned around to see what the kids had their attention on.

"Shyla, don't even think about it!" Ms. Baxter murmured.

"Come on, Mom, please, for later?" Shyla begged.

"I'm not getting you no ice cream sandwiches girl, let's go!" Ms. Baxter demanded, anticipating what Shyla wanted.

"Wait, wait, can you give Chelby some money to go back and buy it for me, please, then?" Shyla pleaded.

"You are nuts, girl. Worry about the show!" Shyla's mother responded.

"I'll get it, Ms. Baxter, If you don't mind. Y'all go ahead in and get ready. It's ok," Chelby assured.

"That girl knows Ms. Kaylie doesn't live too far from us. She can get ice cream from her anytime. But thank you, boo. Meet me inside soon as you're done, ok?" Ms. Baxter replied to Chelby.

Ms. Baxter gave Chelby some money as Shyla and she walked into the school. Chelby stood amongst the students in the short line, waiting for her turn to ask for what Shyla had wanted.

"Hey, Ms. Chelby, what can I get you, pretty young lady?" Ms. Kaylie asked.

"Oh, it's not for me. It's for Shyla, but of course, her regular, please," Chelby answered.

"Ok, no problem, coming right up," Ms. Kaylie replied.

As Chelby leaned forward and looked up towards Ms. Kaylie to give her the money, Ms. Kaylie caught a glimpse of Chelby's necklace. "Oh, Chelby, that's beautiful. It looks great on you, too!" Ms. Kaylie mentioned.

"Oh, thank you, my father bought it for me," Chelby replied. Leaning down and forward towards Chelby, Ms. Kaylie's bracelet crawled down her wrist in clear sight of Chelby.

"Wow, that's a beautiful bracelet, Ms. Kaylie. Are those real diamonds?" Chelby asked.

"Actually, they are. Take a look," Ms. Kaylie replied. Chelby felt the bracelet's diamonds with her fingertips as her fingers grazed Ms. Kaylie's wrist and hand as well.

Did I lock that door after I fed her? Ms. Kaylie thought.

Just then, fear flushed Chelby's face. Chelby still had her hand stuck out like she was touching the diamonds as she slowly walked backward until she fell onto the curb of the street behind her. With her mouth open just enough to breathe, the chills flowing throughout her body had nothing to do with the winter cold.

"Are you ok, honey?" Ms. Kaylie asked. Chelby could not form the words needed, but her face had the expression of someone who just seen a ghost. As her mind became preoccupied with her recent thoughts, Ms. Kaylie began to scramble around to get things in order inside of her truck.

"Sorry, kids, I have to go. Something just came up," Ms. Kaylie explained before walking to the front of the truck.

"Awe, man!" two boys shouted simultaneously.

"See y'all later," Ms. Kaylie mumbled as she left abruptly, waving her hand out the truck window. A young boy turned down towards Chelby to ask if she needed help, extending his hand, but Chelby refused. She wiped herself off, getting up, shaking her head slowly from side to side.

Chelby strolled into the school, looking at the ground, trying to figure out the rush of thoughts that recently filled her head. Chelby began to replay it back over and over in her mind. She saw a girl locked in a room with the TV on. In front of that girl was a table with a plate, fork, cup, and napkin on it. The face of the girl was from the news. It was six-year-old Leila Phillips, the very same little girl that had been missing for a few weeks now.

Chelby couldn't make sense of her thoughts. *What did this mean? How could this be?* As she walked into the school and then into the auditorium where Shyla was performing, she became even more distracted by her thoughts. She almost mistakenly sat in a different row from where Ms. Baxter was seated.

"Hey honey, over here!" Shyla's mother shouted, waving to her from her seat.

"Oh, ok, I'm coming," Chelby responded with an embarrassing smile.

Chelby had to say excuse me at least seven times as she went from one seat to the next, making her way towards Ms. Baxter. She finally got to where Ms. Baxter was and sat down awkwardly.

"Is everything ok, honey? You look pale, sick even?" Ms. Baxter mentioned as she looked Chelby over.

"Um, yeah, I feel a little funny, but I'll be ok, Ms. Baxter. Thank you," Chelby replied.

Chelby would watch her talented friend dance gracefully as the crowd cheered her and the other dancers on in the performance. She would see Ms. Baxter jump out of her seat from time to time, clapping as she smiled from ear to ear. But her vision and hearing were tainted by her thoughts. It was as if her vision was blurred, and her thoughts were muffling the sounds of the music and crowd. She was unable to focus on anything other than her thoughts.

Once the show was over, everyone in the audience, including Chelby, stood up to cheer on the show's dancers as they bowed to the crowd. Chelby smiled as she looked onto Shyla in the distance, who was still breathing heavily from her performance.

Those in attendance began to move out of their seats to either exit or greet the performers who were still on stage. Ms. Baxter grabbed Chelby's hands and hustled along with the crowd as the two went up to congratulate Shyla.

She did so well! Ms. Baxter thought.

"Yeah, she did great, Ms. Baxter!" Chelby said.

"She did, didn't she?" Ms. Baxter replied.

They both gave Shyla a long hug as all three of them embraced at once.

I'm so glad Chelby made it, Shyla thought.

My baby is a star! Ms. Baxter thought.

"Ok, let me go dry off and get changed," Shyla mentioned. "That dress is so pretty, Chelby. I didn't get to really see it outside. Love the necklace too," Shyla added.

For a brief moment, before Shyla spoke of the necklace, the missing little girl wasn't consuming Chelby's thoughts. The visuals of Ms. Kaylie and Leila came flooding back into Chelby's mind again.

"Thank you, Shyla. Go, get dressed. I'll be waiting for you outside, ok," Chelby said.

"I'm starving. Let me get one of those ice cream sandwiches, please," Shyla requested. Both Ms. Baxter and Chelby shook their heads as Chelby handed her one of the sandwiches. "Thanks, see y'all in a second," Shyla responded. Chelby and Ms. Baxter walked out of the auditorium to the front of the gymnasium, where the dance was being held. Kids were already filing in as the two waited for Shyla and the other students from the dance performance to get ready.

"They did so well, didn't they? I was so excited; I rushed out of the house without my camcorder," Ms. Baxter mentioned.

"That's ok, Ms. Baxter, but they did do great. I never knew Shyla was so good!" Chelby replied.

Just then, some of the girls started walking in the dance with Shyla in the middle of the pack. "Oh, that dress is beautiful Shyla, red looks great on you," Chelby exclaimed. Shyla's dress was a red surplice neck self-tie flare dress that looked beautiful under the gymnasium dim fluorescent lights.

"Thank you, Chelby. Ok, let's go in," Shyla replied.

"Ok, I'll be outside when it's over, have fun, girls!" Ms. Baxter said.

The girls waved goodbye to Ms. Baxter as they walked into the gymnasium. The school staff decorated the gym nicely in a prom type of setting. With food, drinks, and a live DJ, you couldn't tell that this was a gym during the week.

"Wow, Chelby, it's nice in here, right?" Shyla mentioned.

Chelby agreed with Shyla and responded, "Yeah, it is... real nice!" The girls were in one section of the gym, while most of the boys scattered about in small groups in different gym areas.

The DJ had all the kids moving their heads. Some boys would try to dance with the girls early on, but the young ladies would rather dance within their all-girl groups. As time passed, both the girls and boys at the dance became more comfortable and began to dance with one another. One of the girls that were bold enough to approach the boys was Shyla, empowering some of the other female students to follow suit. Chelby stood to herself mostly, with her thoughts still surrounding the little girl's whereabouts.

"Come on, Chelby, let's go in the middle," Shyla told Chelby.

Chelby smiled and shyly waved her off before saying, "Nah, I'm good. You go, though."

All the kids were having a great time, but Chelby couldn't ignore her thoughts from earlier. Chelby wondered what she should do next, how she should go about it, and if she should do anything at all.

As the dance came to an end, Chelby and Shyla started walking out of the gym to the school's front. Shyla's mother was waiting for the girls outside. Both Chelby and Shyla walked to the car and got in.

"So, did you have fun, girls? Did y'all dance?" Ms. Baxter asked.

"Well, you know I did, Mom, but Chelby was acting all shy," Shyla replied.

"What happened sweety, you didn't like the dance?" Ms. Baxter asked.

"No, it was fun. I wasn't in the dancing mood as much, though, that's all," Chelby admitted.

"Well, I'm glad y'all had fun, for the most part, and the both of you ended up looking so pretty, too," Ms. Baxter said.

"Oh, thanks Mom!" Shyla replied.

"Thank you, Ms. Baxter, "Chelby responded.

They left the school and went home for the night.

Once Chelby got home, Mia was waiting for her excitedly at the door.

"So how was your first dance baby, did you have a great time?" Mia asked.

"Yeah, it was nice, and Shyla did so well in her performance, too," Chelby replied. Chelby looked down and away from her mother, still being consumed by her frightening thoughts.

"I'm so happy you had a good time. I knew you would," Mia replied. Chelby smirked as she nodded in agreement. "Something happened Chelby, what's wrong?" Mia asked.

Chelby, still looking off in the distance, responded, "Oh nothing, Mom, I guess I'm just a little tired."

"A little tired nothing, something happened, what's wrong?" Mia asked again.

"Nah, just something on my mind. I'm ok," Chelby replied.

Mia slowly approached Chelby and put two of her fingers under her chin to lift her head. "Baby, look at me, please tell me what's on your mind," Mia pleaded.

"Mom, I think I know what happened to that girl," Chelby responded.

Mia looked confused. "What girl, Chelby?"

"You remember the girl that went missing a few weeks back, that one, from the news?" Chelby replied.

"Of course, honey, but what about her?" Mia asked.

"I'm trying to tell you, Mom. I think I know what happened to her and who took her," Chelby responded.

"What, how, who?" Mia confusingly asked. "Ok, so theirs a woman, an ice cream truck driver, that comes in the neighborhood by our school, right," Chelby continued as Mia listened. "She's a nice woman and always nice to the students, but today when she sold ice cream to some of the kids and me, I was able to read her thoughts. When she gave me the ice cream sandwiches for Shyla in front of the school before the show, I was able to read her thoughts," Chelby explained.

"So, what happened, Chelby?" Mia eagerly asked.

"Well, when we touched, I saw a picture of the little girl Leila from the news locked in a room, in my head, with food on a plate in front of her," Chelby admitted.

"What, are you serious? Were you able to see where she was located?" Mia asked.

"No, but before the little girl flashed in my mind, Ms. Kaylie was worried if she fed her or not. She questioned herself, trying to remember if she fed her before she rushed off," Chelby explained.

"Oh my God, that poor little girl, locked up somewhere scared!" Mia exclaimed.

"What should I do, Mom? I don't know what to do," Chelby responded.

"Baby, it's what we're going to do. You're not in this by yourself," Mia replied. "When your father gets home, we'll talk more about it, but you should go get some sleep," her mother instructed.

"Ok, thanks Mom, love you, goodnight," Chelby responded, walking to the bathroom.

"Love you too, Chelby, go get some rest. We'll work it out tomorrow," Mia replied. Chelby listened and felt relieved to speak about what was troubling her.

After her shower, she went straight to bed. It was a long day of events that physically but mostly emotionally drained her. Chelby knocked out as soon as she hit her bed.

When Marcus got home that night while Chelby was sound asleep, both parents discussed with one another what they should do about the possible outcomes of their daughter's latest ability. They went back and forth for the remainder of the night on the pros and cons of their beloved daughter's new unique but scary gifts. The two were amazed by Chelby's abilities but frightened of what people would do if unfortunately revealed.

The following day while Marcus was at the gym, Chelby went with her mother to pick up some things for the shop. As soon as Marcus finished at the gym, he called Mia to meet up for breakfast at a local diner. Once they all arrived, they began to converse about the horrific situation with the little 6-year-old girl, Leila.

"What's up, Dad? How was the gym?" Chelby asked.

"The gym was great, but I'm starving now," Marcus replied as he looked through the menu.

"So baby, your dad and I were discussing what you told me last night about the ice cream lady," Mia mentioned.

"Yeah, Chelby, I think we need to go to the police with this information," Marcus hesitantly added.

"But Daddy, what are we going to say to them? That I read the ice cream lady's mind, so I know that she has Leila?" Chelby asked.

"I know, I know, I wouldn't even say that. They'd look at us like we were crazy," Marcus admitted. "We have to move fast on this though, we have to try and help bring that little girl home," he added.

"Chelby's right, though, Marcus. We have to come up with a plan that won't affect Chelby at all," Mia replied.

"I agree, Mia, I haven't come up with anything yet, but I will," Marcus assured.

After the three of them finished their brunch, Marcus went home to rest as Chelby and Mia headed to the shop. Once outside the shop, Chelby shockingly noticed that it looked as if there hadn't been any fire at all. The salon was up and running, with customers coming in and out.

As soon as both Chelby and Mia walked in, all the other hairstylist and employees ran up to Chelby to hug her as they said hello. It's been months since they have seen her, so they were genuinely excited, and Chelby was excited to see them as well.

"Hey Chelby! What's up Chelby?" some of the hairdressers said, running up to her. Some just ran up to Chelby, looking her over as they hugged her.

"I missed you guys," Chelby confessed.

Chelby caught up with the shop, telling them about the dance and how school was going. *It was a great day,* Chelby thought.

Later that day, Mia wondered if Chelby wanted her hair done. "Hey Chelby, want your hair washed and dried tonight? It's about that time?" Mia asked. "Um, yeah, that's fine," Chelby hesitantly replied.

Mia tried to make light of the tragic situation to help Chelby with her anxiety surrounding what took place. "I know, baby, bad memories, but look, clear skies tonight," Mia said, smiling, pointing to one of the salon windows.

"I know, Mom, I know. Like you said, just scary memories," Chelby replied.

"It's ok, Chelby, we don't have to, only once you feel comfortable," Mia responded.

"I feel fine, Mom. Let's do it," Chelby replied.

Mia locked the door and turned the closed sign around just in case of any late customers. Chelby loved getting her hair washed, sitting back, and relaxing, but here came the challenging part, going under the hairdryer. Chelby had nightmares about this very moment but still was brave enough to go under.

"You good, Chelby?" Mia asked as Chelby sat under the dryer.

"Yes, I'm good, Mom," Chelby replied. Mia cleaned up and put some things away as Chelby sat underneath the dryer, reading a magazine. Once finished, the awkward anxiety feeling was over.

"Man, your hair grew back nice," Mia mentioned," "Thanks, Mom," Chelby replied as she looked into one of the mirrors.

"So, listen, we can braid your hair when we get home, cool?" Mia said as she finished putting things away. "Chelby, is that good with you?" Mia asked.

In the distance, she saw Chelby slumped over in pain. "Chelby, Chelby?!" Mia screamed, running to Chelby.

"I don't feel so good, Mom. I feel like I have to throw up," Chelby responded. Chelby went down to her knees and growled lightly in pain. The lights in the salon began to flicker as Chelby's faint growls became louder.

"Mommy, it hurts!" Chelby grunted. The lights around the shop began to flicker more but then suddenly stop, going back to normal as if nothing ever happened. Chelby's pain also stopped as she slowly got up from her previous crouched position on the floor.

"Are you ok, baby? Are you alright?" Mia asked as she looked Chelby over.

Chelby took a deep breath before saying, "Yes, I'm better now, Mom."

They both hugged one another as Chelby stood up straight. "You scared me, girl. Let's just get everything and head home.

"Ok, Mom," Chelby agreed.

Mia went to grab her bag to head out as Chelby looked at herself in the mirror. "Hey Mom, I feel kind of weird, like full of energy all of a sudden," Chelby mentioned.

"As long as you feel good, baby," Mia replied, walking towards Chelby with a bag in hand.

"Yes, I feel great, real good, like a surge of energy all of a sudden," Chelby admitted. Mia dropped her bag, settling her eyes onto Chelby as she approached. Things rolled from inside her bag onto the salon new floor as other items bounced off it in the opposite direction.

"Mom, what's wrong? Why do you look like that?" Chelby asked. Chelby could see that her mother's eyes were fixated on something else. Mia took a moment before responding.

"Ch-Chelby.... look down, baby," Mia hesitated to say. Chelby looked down and was utterly shocked at what she saw.

"Ma-Mom, what's happening?" Chelby asked. Chelby was hovering inches from the floor in mid-air and plain sight. Chelby got scared and frantically began to look around on both sides of her to try and figure out how to get down. "Mom!?" Chelby shouted as she started to panic. Just then, she fell back to the floor, and Mia ran and slid to where Chelby landed. "Mom, what just happened?" Chelby asked.

"Chelby, I can't explain what I just saw, but..." Mia whispered. She was unable to finish her statement. They looked at one another, got up, and rushed out of the salon.

With both Chelby and her mother trying to comprehend what they just witnessed, you could hear a pin drop on the way home. The short car ride home was quiet with thoughts. *What just happened? How could it?* and *Why?* were all questions that circled both of their minds?

Once they arrived in front of the apartment, they both went to embrace one another. Mia looked down at Chelby and kissed her on the forehead as Chelby's embrace seemed to tighten around Mia's waist.

"I love you, Chelby. I don't understand everything that's going on, but just know, we'll get through this together," Mia stated.

"I know, Mom, and I love you too. It'll be ok," Chelby replied. The two of them walked up to the front of the door as Mia fingered through her keys to locate the right one.

"Don't worry, Mom, Daddy will have some answers, you'll see," Chelby assured.

Mia's eyebrows raised a little as she took a brief moment before saying, "I hope so, Chelby. I hope so."

Chapter 6

Abilities

Mia and Chelby rushed into the apartment, startling Marcus out of sleep. They were both shouting, making it difficult to understand one from the other.

"Wait, wait, wait, what happened?" Marcus confusingly asked, jumping out of bed and running to the living room. Marcus's heart was racing as he tried to make out what the two of them were saying.

His initial concern for their safety slowly went away as Marcus rubbed his eyes, trying to wake up fully. He motioned his hands in a downward direction, signifying for both ladies to calm down.

"Are you guys ok? What's…, what's wrong now?" Marcus asked.

"Yes, we're good, Dad, but something crazy just happened," Chelby replied.

"Crazy, like what?" Marcus asked.

"Marcus, you had to see it. It was unbelievable and amazing all at the same time," Mia added.

"Can y'all please just tell me in plain English what's going on?!" Marcus pleaded.

"Ok, Dad, just now at Mom's salon, I was floating in mid-air. Can you believe that?" Chelby replied.

Marcus looked at Mia before responding, "What is this girl talking about?"

"Marcus, you had to see it. It was unbelievable!" Mia responded.

Marcus made a face of disbelief. "Floating, how?" he asked.

"As I told you, Dad, floating, off the floor, in the air, at Mom's salon," Chelby said. Mia slowly nodded her head several times in agreeance with Chelby as she spoke. "I was so scared at first, trying to figure out what was going on, and seconds later, I was back on the ground again," Chelby explained.

"So, wait, Chelby, you telling me that you were flying around in your mother's salon?" Marcus asked.

"No, Marcus, not flying around, just like...hovering off the floor in one place," Mia tried to explain. Marcus began to rub his head from front to back, then rubbing the back of his head as he looked at both Chelby and Mia. Chelby could tell her father was utterly confused by what was being said to him by both her and her mother.

"Ok, Dad, so, soon after I got from under the dryer, I started to feel a little funny. At first, like, a little sick, then a sudden surge of energy. Right after that, Mom saw me floating off the ground, and I looked down and saw myself inches off the floor, in mid-air," Chelby explained.

After taking a deep breath to inhale, "Wow!" was all Marcus could say after Chelby's explanation. Now with his hand laying on his forehead, Marcus's fingertips slowly grazed back and forth over his eyebrows, as a windshield wiper would under a rain drizzle. As time seemed to stop momentarily, only a few seconds had passed before he spoke again.

"Did anybody see y'all?" Marcus asked.

"I don't think so, Dad," Chelby answered.

"I doubt it, Marcus, and it was late. I don't think anybody was around while we were closing up and getting ready to leave," Mia replied.

"Ok, well, at least that's good. That's good, " Marcus responded. Marcus walked over to Chelby to hug her, patting the top of her head as they embraced. "So, how are you feeling now, Chelby?" Marcus asked.

"I feel pretty good actually, full of energy," Chelby replied.

"Hey, I could use a hug too. What I just witnessed was unbelievable, but it took me right back to that night," Mia admitted.

"Awe, come here, you big baby," Marcus said, as he opened up the embrace he had around Chelby to allow Mia in for a 3-way hug. As they slowly let go, Marcus brushed down the back of Chelby's hair with his hand, and then a thought came to mind.

"So, Mia, as soon as Chelby got up from under the dryer, you saw her hovering in the air?" Marcus asked.

"Well, first, the lights started to flicker some. I forgot to mention that. Then I saw Chelby slumped over in some sort of pain," Mia explained.

"Started to flicker?" Marcus questioned.

"Yeah, Dad, it was kinda weird cause there wasn't a storm outside, but soon after it started, the lights went back to normal," Chelby replied.

"Yeah, that is weird," Marcus agreed. "I wonder... Do you think you can hover right now?" Marcus asked.

"Right now? I don't even know how I did it before," Chelby responded.

"But why, Marcus? What are you thinking?" Mia asked.

"Well, we all agree these abilities have something to do with her hair, right?" Marcus asked. Both Mia and Chelby nodded but stayed quiet. "Well, after hearing about this ability to float or hovering thing y'all both witnessed, there seems to be some sort of connection to the hairdryer as well," Marcus concluded.

Chelby and Mia looked at one another, then back at Marcus to hear the rest of his theory. "I'm no genius or scientist, but it just seems to be connected, somehow," Marcus added.

"Before we make any further assumptions or come to any more conclusions, Chelby, can you please try and hover again?" Marcus asked.

"But how, Dad?" Chelby questioned.

"I don't know, sweety, try and concentrate real hard. Let's see what happens," Marcus replied, as he took a step back.

"Listen, baby; please be careful, stand over by the carpet in the living room, just in case," Mia instructed. Mia pointed towards the small couch area where the carpet began and led into the living room. Just in case Chelby was able to hover again and fell, only the small sofa, along with the carpet underneath, would be in her way.

"Ok, Chelby. Try and concentrate," Marcus said.

Chelby took a deep breath and started to focus. She ignored the faint glow that was coming from underneath her shirt. She winced some and then scratched where the tree-like-shaped mark sat on her arm. The glow went away as Chelby let out a light muffled growl, wincing a little more now than she did prior before. The lights in the kitchen hallway and the living room began to flicker some. As abruptly as they began to flicker off and on, they stopped. Clenching her fist tightly, Chelby threw her hand down onto the edge of the small couch, flipping it over accidentally.

Chelby took a few steps back, as did Marcus and Mia, leaving all three standing there in awe. Chelby held both hands in front of her as if something wasn't right. Marcus was first to notice that her hands, arms, and head were becoming transparent as he hesitantly raised his hand to point in her direction. She was becoming invisible and back visible again, over and over, which almost seemed to happen simultaneously.

"What's happening?!," Chelby whispered. The transparency of her body was now evident, but what happened next left her parents speechless. Both Mia and Marcus' eyes looked at Chelby's feet, fixated, with their mouths open. Chelby looked down, and in amazement, she was hovering over the carpet with her head almost touching the bottom of the living room ceiling light.

What in the world is going on? Marcus thought as he reached to grab her out of mid-air.

"I don't know, Dad! I don't know!" Chelby yelled, panicking and suddenly falling back onto the floor.

"Chelby, Chelby!" Marcus shouted, rushing over to where Chelby fell onto the floor.

"Chelby?!" Mia screamed, reaching out towards her. Marcus held Chelby in his arms while on the floor next to her.

"Are you ok, baby?" Marcus asked as Mia stood over him and Chelby.

"Uh, yeah, I'm good Dad, I just feel so weak," Chelby admitted. Marcus helped stand Chelby up and walked her over to the dining room table to sit. Mia hurried over to the fridge to get some juice to pour for Chelby.

"Here you go, sweetie, drink some," Mia instructed, giving Chelby the Tropicana watermelon flavored juice she had just poured for her.

"Thanks, Mom," Chelby said as she took a sip. After panting from swallowing three quick gulps of the juice, Chelby put the cup down and tried to gather herself.

"Thirsty, huh?" Marcus asked. Chelby slowly nodded her head, yes.

"So how do you feel now, Chelby?" her mother asked.

"I feel ok, Mom, just still weak, a little better than before, though," Chelby replied.

"Weak, how?" Marcus asked.

"Well, kind of similar to how you feel when you have the flu, like achy, with low energy, that's how I feel," Chelby explained. Chelby got up from the dining room table and headed to the couch to lay down. "I feel kinda hot, Mom," Chelby said as she slowly closed her eyes and opened them up again. Mia rushed to the bathroom to get a cloth to wet. She ran it under cold water, rang it out, and hustled back to the living room to put the cold rag on Chelby's forehead.

"She's feeling warm," Marcus whispered to Mia. Mia rushed back into the bathroom to locate the thermometer. Once finding it, she ran back to Chelby to check her temperature. "What does it say, Mia," Marcus asked.

"Give me a second," Mia replied. The thermometer read 101° Fahrenheit, which worried both parents. "Drink the rest of your juice, Chelby, and let me take you to bed so you can get some rest," Marcus instructed. Mia handed Chelby her cup of juice while Marcus sat her up to drink it.

Chelby's eyes were barely open as Marcus carried her to her room. "Leave the rag on your neck baby, it'll help keep you cool," Marcus told Chelby as he helped tuck her in.

"Ok, Dad," Chelby replied.

Marcus stood over Chelby as her eyes began to close, praying, and hoping that she was ok. Marcus prayed in a light whisper that she slept well and felt better by morning.

Mia briefly cleaned up the living room and peeked down the hallway at Marcus to check on Chelby.

"Is she ok?" Mia whispered to Marcus from down the hall.

"Yeah, I think so. She's sleeping now," Marcus responded.

While Mia was scattering around to clean up the living room, Marcus had a flashback to when Chelby was born as he stood over her, observing her sleep. Marcus thought back to the first moment Chelby was introduced to the world through God's blessings. The most beautiful thing Marcus ever laid eyes on, he thought, *so precious, a true gift from God*. Marcus also vividly remembered that immediately after Chelby was born, she was whisked away to the NICU because of trouble breathing.

Although she had tubes in her and monitors around her, she continuously gave him and Mia the most beautiful smiles. He kept saying to himself that Chelby was such a fighter. Marcus felt even then that she was special. Not unique in a sense just for them, but for the world, because she was fighting to be here. Once Mia finished up, she headed for Chelby's room to visually check on her before both she and Marcus went to bed.

While both in bed, neither Mia nor Marcus could sleep. "I can't stop thinking about all that happened tonight. Are you awake, Marcus?" Mia whispered.

"Yeah, I've been thinking the same thing, "Marcus replied as he rolled over to face Mia.

"I'm worried about Chelby. She was so out of it this time," Mia mumbled.

Marcus let out a big sigh before speaking. "Yeah, I know," Marcus responded.

"What do you think that's about? She didn't feel like this the few other times this has happened," Mia questioned.

"Yeah, I know," Marcus repeated, as he stared off into the hallway.

"So, what do you think, Marcus? You keep saying yeah, I know, but what do you think is the problem this time?" Mia asked with frustration.

Marcus took a deep inhale as he laid there in thought before giving Mia an answer. "Did you see Chelby going in and out of invisibility?" Marcus asked.

"Of course, I did. I was standing right there!" Mia replied.

"That was right after she flipped the couch over by banging on it with one hand, and right before she started to hover off the floor in mid-air," Marcus reminded.

"Yes, I know Marcus, so what do you think happened this time? That's what I'm asking," Mia questioned.

"There was something else too, right before she fell, she said, 'I don't know Dad! I don't know,'" Marcus mentioned.

"So?" Mia asked, waiting for a better explanation.

"Mia, when she was hovering, and I reached out to grab her, I thought to myself, what is going on, but I didn't say anything, she read my thoughts is what I'm trying to tell you," Marcus explained.

Mia looked confused and frustrated, trying to understand what Marcus was trying to convey. "Marcus, what does that all mean? She's done all this before," Mia replied.

"Exactly, Mia, she's done that before, just not all at once," Marcus responded.

"I'm confused. So, Marcus, what in the world does that have to do with her feeling this way now?" Mia asked.

"Ok, so...she's displayed extra strength, able to become invisible, able to read minds, and now, sort of fly, correct?" Marcus reminded.

"O...K...?" Mia answered in frustration.

"Cool, so, she's done all of those things on different occasions, but not all at one time, right?" Marcus asked.

"Yeah, that's true," Mia replied.

"See, so this time she could do every ability she has done before on separate occasions, all together, back-to-back," Marcus responded.

"Wow, you're right!" Mia mumbled.

"I think since she did every ability back-to-back as we saw, she became extremely fatigued and weak from doing all of them in one day," Marcus explained.

"How do you think she was able to do all these abilities at once, though, Marcus? She hasn't been able to do that prior till today?" Mia asked.

"As I said before, it has to be connected somehow to her hair, and now it seems to the dryer as well," Marcus responded.

It took a second to digest everything that Marcus said before Mia responded. "So, you think after she was done with the dryer, she was able to use every ability?" Mia asked.

"Yeah, I think so. See, usually, once her hair is dry at home, you braid it, and a new ability happens. This time you left it out, and all her abilities were available to her," Marcus explained.

"Wow, that kinda does make sense. Kinda... I guess," Mia replied. "So, using all of her abilities in the same time frame wiped her out? Is that what you're saying?" Mia questioned.

"Yeah, that's what I was thinking. She's never been like this before because, before tonight, she was only able to use one ability at one time," Marcus concluded.

"Wow, you're much smarter than you look, sometimes," Mia replied with a grin.

"Oh, why thank you. I try!" Marcus responded, smiling as well.

"I just hope she's ok, that's all," Mia declared.

Marcus brought Mia closer and kissed her on the side of her face. "Yeah, so do I, Mia, but she'll be fine. I know she will. Get some rest, babe, love you, goodnight," Marcus said.

"Good night, love you too," Mia responded. They kissed one another goodnight before rolling over to fall asleep.

The following day while both Mia and Chelby slept, Marcus got ready for work. He would generally be up and out on the road hours before the two even would open their eyes for the day. On this morning, Marcus went to check on Chelby thoroughly before heading out. Once he entered Chelby's room, he noticed that she was all covered up, with her covers draped over her head. Marcus immediately found this to be weird because Chelby's room was warm. Marcus slowly pulled back the covers and noticed that Chelby was sleeping in the fetal position and sweat that seemed to be dripping from her forehead drenched her pillowcase and tee shirt as well. Marcus could tell she was vividly dreaming from her eyes moving around while closed.

"Chelby," Marcus whispered. Chelby just moaned and rolled over without waking up. Marcus hurried to the kitchen to pour some water. He turned on a hallway light that woke Mia up in the process. As he reached to get a cup for Chelby, he knocked several down into the sink, fully waking Mia up.

"Marcus...Marcus!" Mia whispered down the hall.

"One second," Marcus replied in a low voice. Marcus poured some water into a cup and hustled back with it to Chelby's room, spilling drops of water along the way.

"Chelby, Chelby! Wake up! Drink this!" Marcus demanded in a low but stern tone.

Chelby rolled back onto her other side, facing Marcus. Her mouth was dry, and her throat was sore, which made her respond in a raspy voice. "Daddy?" Chelby said with her eyes still closed. "Dad, what time is it?" Chelby groggily asked.

"Don't worry about that, baby. Just drink this water," Marcus responded.

"Marcus, what's going on?" Mia asked from the other room.

"One second, Mia," Marcus replied. "I'll be right back, baby," he told Chelby.

Marcus left Chelby's room to return to his and Mia's and inform Mia about what was going on. As he reached his doorway, Mia was already up and out of bed, trying to tie her robe together.

"Marcus, what's going on? Is Chelby ok?" Mia questioned.

"I think she's running a fever; her shirt and pillow were full of sweat, but she seemed to still be cold," Marcus replied.

Mia didn't think twice. She flew down the hallway into the bathroom to find the thermometer to bring back for Chelby. She didn't even bother turning on the light. Mia knew roundabout where the thermometer was, grabbed it, and rushed back to Chelby. Chelby's temperature read 102.5°.

"What was it again last night?" Marcus asked.

"It was 101. Should we take her to the doctor?" Mia answered.

"I want to go to school, Mom," Chelby mumbled.

"Forget about school right now, Chelby. We have to get you feeling well again. Drink the rest of your water, please," Marcus demanded. Chelby nodded her head and finished whatever water was left in her cup. After wiping her mouth, she turned back over, pulling the covers over her body to stay warm.

"Baby, I'm right here outside your room if you need me, ok," Marcus said while motioning for Mia to follow him into the hallway.

"Uh-huh," Chelby mumbled.

Mia acknowledged Marcus and followed him into the hallway. "I think we need to take her to the hospital Marcus, she looks weak, and her temperature has risen from last night," Mia explained in a low voice, trying not to disturb Chelby.

"I know, I know, but let's just see once she's rested if her fever comes down some," Marcus responded.

"Well, obviously she can't go to school today, so are you staying home with her? Remember today those contractors are coming back by the shop. It might be an all-day thing today, too," Mia admitted.

"Of course, let me call the job now to tell them Chelby is sick and that I'm not coming in today. I'll just let them know that I have to stay home with her," Marcus replied.

"Ok, I'm gonna go get some Tylenol from the bathroom for Chelby while you do that. It'll help keep her temperature down," Mia responded.

Marcus went into the living room to call his job as Mia went to get the Tylenol for Chelby. While Marcus was still on the phone with his job, Mia woke Chelby back up to give her the Tylenol.

"Chelby..., Chelby?" Mia whispered, trying to wake Chelby up. Chelby moaned, then rolled over to face Mia with her eyes barely open.

"Huh, what, it's time for school already, Mom?" Chelby asked.

"No, baby, you're not going to school today, but take this," Mia instructed, handing Chelby the Tylenol from one hand while holding a cup of water in the other.

"Come on, Mom?" Chelby grunted.

"Girl, this is going to take your temperature down! And drink this. All of it!" Mia demanded, handing Chelby the cup. Chelby drank all of the water and gave the cup back to her mother with her eyes closed, then rolled back over.

"Feel better, Chelby," Mia whispered as she kissed Chelby on the back of her head.

After Marcus ended the call with his job, he got up from the couch and headed back to Chelby's room. "You gave her the Tylenol already?" Marcus asked in a low tone.

"Yes, I did," Mia answered. Marcus briefly looked at Chelby and turned his attention back to Mia.

"I have to get..." Before Mia could finish, Marcus hustled to the bathroom. He got some tissue and brought it back to Chelby's room.

"I'm sorry, babe, what were you saying?" Marcus asked as he wiped the sweat off Chelby's forehead with the tissue.

"No, I was just saying that I have to get up in an hour to open up the shop, so I'm going to go lay back down for a few," Mia explained.

"Of course, go ahead, try and get a little more rest if you can. I got her, " Marcus responded.

"Ok," Mia replied. Mia rubbed Chelby's back twice before leaving, giving Marcus a loving look as she exited Chelby's room.

"She'll be fine, babe," Marcus whispered to Mia as Mia headed back to bed.

Once Mia laid back down, Marcus went to the living room to take off his work clothes and turn on the TV. He put the sports channel on, but on low, to make sure not to disturb both his favorite ladies. Marcus got up to get a drink and heard Mia snoring from down the hallway.

Man, she must have been tired. It sounds like a chainsaw in there, he chuckled and thought to himself.

Almost two hours had passed when Mia's alarm went off for her to get up and ready for work. She hit the snooze button the first time, and 5 minutes later, Marcus heard her slowly get out of bed.

"Morning, Mia. Hey, it sounded like you were chopping trees in that room last night!" Marcus joked. Mia didn't even look down the hallway to acknowledge Marcus. She went straight into the bathroom. That made Marcus laugh because he knew Mia wasn't a morning person. Once Mia got out of the shower, she briefly checked on Chelby, kissed her, and rushed to get dressed.

"So, listen, make sure you check on Chelby periodically, and I think you should give her some oatmeal and more Tylenol when she gets up," Mia directed, scattering around getting dressed. "Recheck her temperature soon as she gets up, and if it's higher than what it already is or hasn't dropped any, take her to the ER," Mia demanded.

"Listen, listen, Mrs., I got this. You think I can't take care of my own daughter?" Marcus asked.

"Our daughter! And yes, of course, you can, but you heard what I said to do, right?" Mia responded.

"Yes, ma'am, I did," Marcus answered, shaking his head. "Ok, I'm running late. I'll see you later. Love you. Bye," Mia said, rushing out the door.

"Love you too. Be safe," Marcus responded.

Soon as Mia locked the door behind her, Marcus got up off the couch to check on Chelby. Her forehead was still moist with sweat, so he went back into the bathroom for more tissue and a washcloth. From the bathroom, Marcus could hear Chelby moan and toss in her bed. He walked back into Chelby's room to wipe her forehead again. Chelby rolled, following up with muffled moaning.

Marcus left Chelby and headed into the dining room to get a chair to bring back to Chelby's room. He wanted to sit down to watch over her carefully. She seemed to be having a bad dream. Marcus didn't know for sure, but he had a feeling he was right. She began to moan louder as her eyelids moved back and forth more aggressively.

Chelby seemed to slowly reach for something as her lips tried to form words. She gasped and suddenly woke up. Once she realized she was awake, looking directly into her father's eyes, tears slowly began to flow down her cheeks.

"Baby, are you ok? What's wrong?" Marcus asked. Marcus got up from the chair he brought into Chelby's room and sat alongside her to comfort her. Chelby sat up, still with tears flowing, trying to make out what she just dreamt. She began to shake her head while in deep thought before she spoke.

Chelby took a deep breath and wiped her tears. "I was walking in this desert, alone, the sun was bright, and it was hot. I could actually feel the heat, Dad, and I could feel the sand go across my face when a gust of wind would blow. It seemed like I was walking for hours, and I began to struggle walking in the sand," she sighed before continuing. "Then it suddenly got dark, but not pitch black. The moon's light was just as bright as the sun, and in the distance, I could see trees in a small section of the desert where I was walking. As I got closer, lightning began to flash around the trees, without any sound of thunder, lighting up the night sky with each strike. The sky was a different color than I've ever seen it; it was a beautiful purple or violet color only made visible by the flashes of lightning.

"The closer I approached, I could tell that this section of the desert was an oasis because I could smell the water the closer I got to the trees. I could see the lightning flash vividly around the oasis, big flashes of light, each rigid curve, and detail of the lightning I could see, but I wasn't scared. As I made my way up to the trees, there was a short path from the desert into the oasis where the water was. I walked through the path to get to the water, and I made it through. It was beautiful inside the oasis, with tropical trees, flowers, and plants surrounding the water. The colors were vibrant and drew my attention. I could still see the lightning, but it was on the outside of the oasis. I heard a female's voice on the other side of the water but couldn't make out what she was saying. I began to get closer to the edge of the water so I could see who she was. When I did this, her words got louder and clearer as well. She was yelling, '*Help, help, I'm over here!*' It seemed like she was trying to get across but couldn't.

"I was too far away from her, and she was too far away from me. As I looked closer at the girl's face, it was the girl from the news, Leila, just older, about my age. I couldn't speak. I just reached out. She started to sink in the sand as I reached out to her and as she reached out to me. Before she fully was covered by the sand, I woke up," Chelby concluded.

Marcus' eyes grew wide. He initially didn't know how to respond. He brought Chelby closer into his arms as Chelby's head laid in his chest. He kissed her on top of the forehead and wiped away the remaining tears on her face.

"Wow, that's an incredible dream you just had," Marcus mentioned.

Chelby sat back up on her bed before saying, "I know, Dad, but what do you think it means?" Marcus paused for a moment, gently biting the inside of his mouth, trying to gather his thoughts to give Chelby the correct answer.

"Well, Chelby, it's like this, sometimes dreams are just dreams, but other times they can mean something," Marcus replied. "Ok, Dad, so now both you and my dream are confusing me," Chelby responded.

Before he could finish his thought, Marcus's cell phone went off, he could hear it, but it wasn't in the room with him and Chelby. He had left it somewhere in the living room. "Give me a second. That's probably your mother checking up on you. I'll be right back," Marcus said, hurrying to the sound of his phone. The phone was on the floor in front of the couch.

Once picking it up, he realized that he was right. It was Mia texting to check up on Chelby. Marcus texted Mia back, got some water for Chelby, and hurried back into Chelby's room.

"Was it, Mom?" Chelby asked.

"Yeah, it was your mother, asking how you were doing," Marcus replied.

"Drink this," Marcus said as he gave Chelby the water he just poured while in the kitchen.

"Ok, so what was I saying?" Marcus asked, scratching his head as he sat back down onto Chelby's bed.

"You were trying to confuse me more about this dream," Chelby replied. Marcus smiled before he spoke.

"Yes, so, you ever had a dream about someone that you know or seen before, and somehow y'all cross paths in a familiar place in your dream?" Marcus asked.

"Yeah..." Chelby responded.

"Right, that's a typical dream to have. We've all had it. At times most of us can't remember every detail of the dream, but that's normal," Marcus replied. "Now, have you ever had a dream about swimming or something about water, and you suddenly wake up because you have to use the bathroom?" Marcus asked.

"Yes, definitely... I hate those dreams," Chelby replied. Marcus laughed.

"I know, but subconsciously, your brain is telling you information about things around you, through your senses involving your dreams. It could have been a fly next to your ear, but in your dream, it's a helicopter flying overhead. Or the scent of your mother making dinner, but in your dream, you're eating at a Barbecue somewhere, get it?" Marcus explained.

"Yes, that's true," Chelby admitted.

"But sometimes, and this is extremely rare and may never happen to most, there's something profound about the dream, and the person can vividly recall every detail within that dream. Now that's usually a message from God," Marcus exclaimed.

"A message from God?" Chelby questioned.

"I confused you again, didn't I?" Marcus asked with a smirk on his face, as Chelby nodded. Chelby sipped some more of the water her father brought for her, awaiting more explanation on what he just stated. "Ok, so... God can be different things for different people. By the way, I don't know everything about God and may never," Marcus said as he continued. "Different religions have different names and foundational beliefs for Him. With that said, most equally believe in a creator of all things and of all people. You follow so far?" Marcus asked.

"Yeah, I know, I follow," Chelby replied.

"Ok, so, the Creator, God, can be both simple and complex. He can be both direct and indirect," Chelby's face had an expression of confusion again. Her father smiled and said, "Let me further explain. At times, God can present two clear choices to you, either you go right, and this happens, or you go left, and that happens. Easy to figure out and easy to understand. From my experience and knowledge, He doesn't do this by verbally saying this, but by presenting a situation in front of you, forcing you to make a clear and decisive choice. Understand so far?" Marcus asked.

"Yes...," Chelby responded, nodding.

"Now, there are those extraordinary times he conveys his message through a dream for us to decipher or decode, and that's what I believe He has done with you," Marcus said.

"But why, Dad, why me?" Chelby asked.

"That's the wrong question Chelby, we honestly may never understand why to most things when concerning God, but we must figure out what the message is and how to fulfill what He wants concerning that message," Marcus explained.

Chapter 7

Sidekick

"So, Dad, what do you think the message is?
What do you think God is trying to tell me?" Chelby
asked. "As I said, it's not going to be 100 percent clear of
what He wants all the time. It's kind of like putting a
puzzle together with the pieces mixed up in front of us.
We have to put it together on our own," Marcus
explained.

"Ok, I understand. I get that," Chelby replied.

"One big piece of the puzzle in your dream was the fact that you saw an older version of the kidnapped girl Leila in it," Marcus mentioned.

"I know, Dad, that was crazy! She started to sink into the sand, reaching out for me. That part was terrifying," Chelby added.

"I know, that would have been scary for me too," Marcus admitted.

"Scary for you, but you're not scared of anything, Dad," Chelby responded.

"No, that's not true, but scary because I couldn't help her, but I would want to, that's what I meant," Marcus explained.

"Oh, yeah, I understand. Well, maybe that's what the message was, that I have to help Leila before it's too late," Chelby replied.

"Yeah, that's what I think to" Marcus mumbled.

Marcus brought Chelby closer to him with his arm around her waist and whispered, "Don't worry, we'll figure this out together."

Chelby slowly nodded her head in agreeance but with thoughts of uncertainty. Marcus helped Chelby up and slowly walked her to the bathroom to wash up. "Do you need help washing?" Marcus asked.

"Dad, I'm not dying, don't be crazy. Close the door, please!" Chelby directed.

"Ok, ok, sorry, just asking," Marcus replied with an embarrassing look on his face. Marcus was making his way towards the kitchen, stopped halfway, and walked back to the hallway bathroom. He knocked softly on the bathroom door before asking, "Chelby, what do you want for breakfast?"

"Can you just make me some oatmeal, please," Chelby asked.

"Sure, baby, you don't want any sausage or bacon with that?" Marcus asked.

"No, just oatmeal is fine, thanks, Dad," Chelby replied. Marcus continued back to the kitchen to fix breakfast as Chelby continued washing up in the bathroom.

At times, she would close her eyes while brushing her teeth, and every time she would do this, flashes of lightning from her dream would pop up in her head. She quickly would open her eyes and look in the mirror to reassure herself that it wasn't real. Chelby hopped in the shower and let the warm water run off the back of her neck. She closed her eyes to relax some, but in doing this, flashes of the vivid dream popped up again. This time she saw the oasis clearly and young Leila sink into the sand before opening her eyes again.

She turned off the water, got out to dry off, and headed to her room to get dressed. "Chelby, you good?" Marcus asked, yelling down the hallway.

"Yes, I'm ok, just getting dressed," Chelby responded, yelling back down the hall from her room. Once dressed, Chelby headed to the dining room to eat. Although she still felt achy with chills, Chelby was starving, which was a good sign, it meant that she still had her appetite.

"Do you want bananas cut up in your oatmeal?" Marcus asked.

"Oh, yes, please, thank you," Chelby replied, sitting down at the table. Marcus cut up the bananas and evenly spread them around the oatmeal, placing the bowl in front of Chelby before sitting down to eat. "Hmm, you always make the best oatmeal, Dad," Chelby said after eating two spoonsful.

"Do I? I'm glad you like it," Marcus responded. "Listen, please take that Tylenol I left next to your cup. Your mother will kill me if I didn't make you take it,"

Marcus explained. Chelby listened and took the Tylenol. "So, how are you feeling?" Marcus asked.

"So, so. I'm still a little achy like I was in a wrestling match or something," Chelby explained.

"Yeah, you might have to take a few days off from school, just to recover and get back to your normal self," Marcus cautioned.

"Uh-huh," Chelby replied reluctantly.

Chelby began to stare off as she ate the oatmeal, a telltale sign that she was in deep thought. "Chelby, are you ok? What you thinking about, and don't tell me nothing cause I know that look?" Marcus demanded. Chelby took a deep breath before she responded.

"Well, Dad, in the bathroom just now, I was having flashes of that dream I just had, and I guess I was thinking about that," Chelby admitted.

"Oh, yeah, I could tell something was bothering you," Marcus responded.

"Dad, we have to find little Leila, somehow, someway," Chelby emphatically stated.

"I know, baby, I know, I believe we will," Marcus replied. "Wait, Chelby, I almost forgot," Marcus said, getting up from the table. Marcus headed to the bathroom and came back to the dining room with the thermometer.

"If I don't check your temperature and text your mother the results, she'll be worried all day!" Marcus admitted. Chelby's temperature was back down to 101°, still higher than average but lower than earlier that morning. "Ok, a little better than this morning, at least. Let me text your mother real quick," Marcus said as he put the dishes into the sink. After putting his phone back in his pocket, Marcus sat back down with Chelby.

"Did you get through to Mom?" Chelby asked.

"Well, she didn't respond yet. She's probably busy at the shop," Marcus replied. "Listen, we need to discuss how and why you are feeling like this in the first place," Marcus said.

"What do you mean?" Chelby asked.

"What do I mean? Were you there last night, or that was another hovering child of mine?" Marcus asked.

"Well, you did tell me to try it again, Dad, just saying," Chelby answered with a smile.

"No, you're right, I did, but that's what I meant. We need to talk about that," Marcus insisted. The vibration of Marcus's phone suddenly drew his attention to his shorts pocket. "This is probably your mother," Marcus said as he took out his phone.

"What's up babe, what happened?" Marcus asked.

"Is she up? How is she doing? Did she eat?" Mia asked at a rushed pace.

"Well, hello to you too, but yes, she's up. I'll let you speak to her yourself," Marcus responded, then gave Chelby the phone.

"Hey, Mom!" Chelby said with a big smile on her face.

"Morning, baby, I was so worried about you. How are you feeling? Did your father feed you?" Mia asked.

"Yes, I ate. I feel a little better but still achy all over," Chelby explained.

"Well, I'm glad you were able to eat something. Make sure you continue to drink a lot of fluids throughout the day as well. That's very important to your temperature coming down. I think you're going to need a couple more days at home to recover, too," Mia explained.

"Ok, Mom, I will," Chelby responded.

"I'll see you when I get home. Feel better, get some rest, and I love you. Give the phone back to Dad, please," Mia instructed.

"Thanks, Mom. I love you too," Chelby replied, handing the phone back to her father.

"Yes..." Marcus said, with his ear to the phone.

"At least she was able to eat something. You gave her the oatmeal?" Mia asked.

"Yes, ma'am, I did. She ate it all too," Marcus replied.

"She said she's still achy though, what was her temperature this time?" Mia asked.

"It was back down to 101° like it was last night. So, it's a little improvement this morning," Marcus replied.

"Ok, good! I gotta go. I'll text you later," Mia responded.

"Ok, be safe. I'll keep you posted," Marcus replied, ending the phone call.

"So, before we were rudely interrupted by your mother, we were just about to speak on the reasoning behind you feeling like this in the first place," Marcus mentioned.

Chelby smirked before saying, "Yeah, I know, I can't remember feeling this down and out, even when I had the flu," Chelby admitted.

"Your mother and I were briefly discussing it last night, and we think it's because you used all of your abilities at once," Marcus responded.

"Yeah, that's probably true, but remember, I wasn't even able to do more than one ability before the other day. So, it's strange that all of a sudden, I can," Chelby admitted. "Very strange; the only thing we came up with is that it must have something to do with the hairdryer and your hair. Now how it's connected, that's a different question we don't have answers to, just yet," Marcus explained. Chelby began to bite the inside of her lip, similar to how her father bites his.

"You know, Dad, every time Mom would do my hair after the fire in the shop, I would be able to do a different ability, right. This time, Mom just washed it and put me under the dryer, and I was able to not only hover but do all of these abilities I did before right after. I think if I leave my hair out after being under the dryer for a while, I'm able to use all these abilities at one time. What do you think, Dad?" Chelby concluded.

"Wow, I think you might be right, but now look what it does to you," Marcus responded.

"Yeah, I know, Dad. This whole thing is just a lot," Chelby replied.

"I know it is, baby," Marcus said.

As they were talking, Chelby began to sweat from her forehead. She moved over to the arm of the couch she and her father were sitting on and rested her head there.

"Ok, baby, it looks like it's time to go back to bed again. You're not looking too good," Marcus mentioned. Chelby wiped the sweat off her head with first the back of her hand then the front of it as her eyes rolled in the back of her head.

"Ok, Dad, thanks for breakfast and everything," Chelby said in a low tone as she got up and walked to her room.

"You're very welcome, always. I'll be in there to check on you soon after I wash these few dishes in the sink," Marcus responded.

Chelby went straight to her bed, and Marcus headed to the kitchen. Once finished with the dishes, he went to check on Chelby to make sure she was ok. Marcus could hear the light snoring coming from Chelby's room as he approached. Marcus thought to himself with a smirk on his face; there's no way she could be asleep already. He was wrong. Chelby was fast

194

asleep. Marcus looked her over, wiping some of the sweat off her forehead, and headed back to the living room to finish watching TV.

A couple of days had passed, with Chelby still recovering, but her father had to go back to work. It was great timing because Chelby was almost back to feeling 100 percent and getting bored staying home by the day. It was late afternoon, and Mia was about to leave her shop early when Shyla walked in the door. "Hey Mrs. Mia, how are you? Can I talk to you real quick?" Shyla asked.

"Hey Shyla, of course, you can, sweetie, give me one second. I was just leaving, ok?" Mia replied.

"Ok," Shyla said eagerly. Mia gathered some things, waved to her employees, and headed out the door with Shyla.

"So how have you been Shyla, what did you have to ask me?"

"I'm good, Mrs. Mia. I was just worried about Chelby. I haven't seen her at school for a few days now. I even called the house, but no one picked up," Shyla explained.

"Oh, you did? That's strange that nobody picked up because Chelby's father has been home with her all week. Chelby hasn't been feeling well since last Friday, so we've been keeping her home," Mia replied.

"Oh man, there's been a stomach thing going around at school too. How is she feeling now?" Shyla asked.

"Oh, she's much better. I'm going home now if you want to come to see her," Mia said.

"Oh, that'll be real cool," Shyla replied.

"Ok, call your mother just to let her know where you're going and where you'll be," Mia instructed as she handed Shyla her phone.

"Ok, thank you, Mrs. Mia," Shyla responded, dialing her mother's number into Mia's phone. Once Shyla's mother gave her the ok, Mia and Shyla headed out. Shyla was excited to surprise her friend.

As Mia was opening the front door to the apartment, she hid Shyla behind her. Marcus, hearing the keys, slowly walked to the door.

"Hey babe, how was your day," Marcus asked.

"It was good, it was good, look who I got here with me," Mia whispered, signaling to Marcus not to reveal who was behind her. Marcus smiled, then called out to Chelby, who was watching TV in her room.

"Hey Chelby, come out here for a second, please," Marcus yelled out. Chelby came out of her room in a hurry.

"What's wrong, Dad? Is everything ok?" Chelby looked around the room. "Oh, hey Mom, I didn't hear you get home," Chelby mentioned.

With a big smile, Mia said, "Hey Chelby, look who I got here with me," Chelby couldn't see Shyla behind her mother's back. Shyla's short stature enabled Mia to hide her at an angle.

"What's up!! What's up!! What's up?!" Shyla shouted, popping out from behind Mia's back.

"What!!! Shyla, what are you doing here?" Chelby shouted. The two girls smiled from ear to ear and hurried to one another to share a hug.

"She came to check on you at the shop, so I asked her to roll with me home so she'd get a chance to see you," Mia said.

"Wow, thanks, Mom!" Chelby replied, still hugging Shyla.

Suddenly Shyla gently pushed Chelby back.

"Wait, your mother told me you were sick. Girl, you still got the cooties?" Shyla asked with a serious look on her face.

"No crazy girl, it wasn't like that," Chelby replied, laughing. Mia started laughing as well while Marcus shook his head back and forth, smiling.

"Listen, girls; y'all can go catch up in Chelby's room as I get dinner ready. Shyla, I'll text your mother to let her know that you're staying for dinner, and Chelby's father will take you home right after, ok?" Mia explained.

"Chelby's father? How I get volunteered?" Marcus murmured.

"Marcus, you can take the girl after dinner," Mia whispered.

"Of course, I can. I was just asking," Marcus whispered back.

Shyla didn't hear the brief conversation between Mia and Marcus. "Ok, thank you, Mr. and Mrs. Williams. I really appreciate that," Shyla responded.

"Come on, girl," Chelby said, tugging on Shyla's shirt.

"You're very welcome, sweetie," Mia responded.

"No problem Shyla," Marcus added. Shyla and Chelby went off to Chelby's room.

The two girls caught up briefly about school while watching TV. "So, what made you come by my mother's shop today?" Chelby asked.

"Dance practice was canceled at the last minute, so I said to myself, let me go check on my girl real quick. I went to the shop and asked your mother about you and asked if you were alright," Shyla responded.

"Oh, that was so nice of you, thank you for doing that," Chelby replied.

"I was hoping to see Ms. Kaylie drive by too. I could've definitely taken down an ice cream sandwich," Shyla mentioned. Chelby's facial expression completely changed. "What's wrong?" Shyla asked.

"Um, nothing, nothing…" Chelby responded in a low tone.

"So, what was wrong with you? You caught that stomach thing that's been going around?" Shyla asked.

"Nah, it wasn't like that," Chelby replied.

"Man, so what was it?" Shyla questioned.

"The food will be ready in about 10 mins guys!" Mia shouted from down the hall.

Chelby got up from her chair in her room to walk a few steps to her doorway.

"Ok, Mom, thank you!" Chelby shouted back. Chelby closed her door some and sat back down across from Shyla.

Shyla could tell something was bothering Chelby. "What's wrong, Chelby? You ok?" she asked. Chelby took a long, deep inhale before slowly letting it out.

"I don't even know where to begin," Chelby responded.

"Spit it out, girl," Shyla said.

"Listen, you can't tell anybody this," Chelby mumbled.

"Anybody what, what are you talking about?" Shyla replied.

"I'm trying to tell you something, but you have to understand that you can't tell anybody, anywhere, at any time, what I'm about to tell you. Do you understand?" Chelby explained.

Shyla rolled her eyes. "No, I don't understand. What in the world are you talking about?" Shyla asked.

"I'm saying, before I say anything else, you have to promise me never to tell anybody what I'm about to tell you now," Chelby demanded.

"You haven't even said anything yet. I'm lost already, but alright, yes, I promise," Shyla responded, getting anxious.

Chelby got up and looked out from her doorway, then proceeded to pace the room. "What is wrong with you girl, you're freaking me out. What do you not want me to tell?" Shyla questioned. Chelby stopped dead in her tracks and looked Shyla in the eyes. "What, Chelby, what is it?" Shyla asked aggressively.

"Well, I kinda have these special... abilities," Chelby said, scratching the back of her head.

Shyla's eyebrows arched with a puzzled look on her face. "Special abilities, like what?" Shyla questioned.

"It's hard to explain, but since the fire at the shop, I've been able to do things I could never imagine doing before," Chelby replied.

"Do things like what though, give me an example," Shyla asked.

"Ok, remember the situation with Billy, how I pushed him, and he flew under the table?"

"Of course, I remember. That was epic!" Shyla replied with a smirk.

"Did you find anything strange about that?" Chelby asked.

"No, not really, you pushed him, and he fell under the table. It was too funny," Shyla mentioned.

"Ok, so the day before that, I was able to push that big couch in the living room all the way down the hall with one push. Then after that, I helped my mother push it back to where it belonged. At one point, she stopped helping me, and I was able to do it by myself with just a few fingers, with hardly any effort at all," Chelby admitted.

"You're talking about that big couch I just passed outside? No way, impossible!" Shyla exclaimed.

"That's what I'm trying to tell you, I did it, though, and the following day I pushed Billy, and he flew across one table and ended up under another," Chelby explained. Shyla looked confused. "That's not it, though," Chelby added. "You know little Cameron, right?" Chelby asked.

"Who that little cutie pie you tutor? Yeah, what about him?" Shyla responded.

"So, between us, he and other students in his class were being mistreated by Mr. Mcintosh. I was able to disappear and secretly record Mr. Mcintosh to prove to Ms. Bell how he treats them," Chelby said.

"Nah, no way! Are you saying that you can become invisible?" Shyla asked.

"You see that he's on suspension now, right? He hasn't been to school in a while, right?" Chelby responded.

"I haven't really notice till now, but now that you've mentioned it, it's true I haven't seen him in a few weeks. Wait, are you saying you're the reason for that?" Shyla asked.

Chelby nodded her head. "That's not all. I've been able to read minds and as crazy as this sounds, as of recently, kind of, hovered off the floor in the air, too," Chelby exclaimed.

"What??? Yo Chelby, have you been taking drugs or something?" Shyla whispered.

"I know, I know, sounds crazy, but it's all true," Chelby admitted.

"Ok, so let's say I'm taking drugs too, and I believe you, how, how are you able to do these things? Can you do something right now?" Shyla asked.

"I tried to explain to you, after the fire, I've been able to do these things. Once I was electrocuted and recovered, I had these abilities. Oh, and it has something to do with my hair, too," Chelby explained.

"Your hair, how?" Shyla questioned.

"I don't know exactly how, but every time my mother does my hair, I can do a different ability. So, I said all of that to explain why I was so sick. A few days ago was the first time I could do all of my abilities at one time. Once I did them all, it took all of the energy out of me, gave me a high temperature, and my body was aching like I had the flu," Chelby explained. Shyla was speechless. "Theirs one more thing," Chelby mentioned.

"One more thing?!" Shyla asked, with her hands on top of her head. Chelby began to pace her room again. "Yeah, you know that little girl that was kidnapped, well..."

"Dinner is ready, girls!" Mia called from the kitchen.

"Little girl, what?" Shyla rushed to ask.

"I'll tell you later," Chelby whispered.

"Coming, Mom!" Chelby yelled from her room. Chelby and Shyla headed to the dining room to eat dinner.

After praying over the food, Marcus took his plate to the loveseat directly in front of the TV, leaving the girls and Mia at the dining room table to eat without him. "What, too many females at one table for you, Marcus?" Mia joked.

"Sure is. I know when I'm outnumbered and when to bow out gracefully," Marcus replied. Chelby and Shyla laughed.

"Dang, Mrs. Williams, this pasta and bread are delicious. It's like an Italian Thanksgiving or something. Thank you!" Shyla mentioned.

"Oh, you're welcome sweetie, I'm glad you're enjoying it," Mia responded, smiling.

"She's so greedy," Chelby said, laughing.

"So, how have you been doing in school, Shyla?" Mia asked.

"Oh, I've been doing real good, just tryna finish strong, you know," Shyla replied.

"I know how that goes, but I'm pleased to hear that you're doing well. Keep pushing, and you will finish strong," Mia encouraged.

The ladies continued to converse over dinner while Marcus couldn't take his eyes off the basketball game that was on TV. Once finished, Shyla offered to wash all the dishes.

"Ok, Marcus, can you please take Shyla home now? It's starting to get late," Mia asked.

"Of course, of course... but give me like 15 minutes please, the fourth quarter just started," Marcus replied.

"Ok, but soon as it's over, please," Mia mentioned.

Marcus was too engulfed in the game to respond. "Marcus?" Mia called. Marcus still didn't answer. "Marcus!" Mia shouted.

"Yes, yes, soon as it's over," Marcus responded.

"Girls, y'all can go back to Chelby's room until this game is over," Mia instructed.

"Ok, Mom," Chelby replied as both she and Shyla headed to Chelby's room.

"Oh, and thank you for washing the dishes, Shyla," Mia shouted from down the hall.

"No problem, Mrs. Williams," Shyla yelled back from Chelby's room.

Chelby turned her TV volume up a little higher than she usually would, hoping that her parents couldn't eavesdrop on the rest of Shyla and her conversation. Shyla quickly sat down on the edge of Chelby's bed. One of her legs began to bounce up and down, showing anticipation for what Chelby had to say next.

"So real quick, before your Dad is ready to take me, what about this little girl, now?" Shyla asked. Chelby sat right next to Shyla so she could talk in a low tone.

"So, you know about the little girl that was kidnapped and has been missing for a few weeks now, right? It's been on the news," Chelby stated.

"Yeah, I remember seeing something about her," Shyla responded with a puzzled look on her face. Chelby took a quick breath to put together her thoughts.

"That day of your performance, when Ms. Kaylie gave me your ice cream beforehand, I was able to see something about her," Chelby mentioned. Shyla's eyes grew wide. "I saw the little girl, Leila, in some room, locked in, and I think Ms. Kaylie has something to do with it," Chelby explained.

"What?! What you mean something to do with it?" Shyla mumbled.

"Shyla, I'm not 100 percent certain of what or how she has something to do with it. I just know she does," Chelby assured.

"But how do you know this? This is insane!" Shyla asked.

"Well, remember I told you, I was able to read minds, well, after my mother did my hair, that's how," Chelby responded.

"Yeah, I remember you saying that, but..." Shyla mumbled. "Well, when we touched as she gave me the ice cream, I was able to read her thoughts, and a picture of the little girl Leila popped in my head. On top of that, as soon as that vision left my thoughts, Ms. Kaylie was thinking or at least trying to remember if she locked the door before she left," Chelby explained.

"Wait, what door?" Shyla asked.

"I think she meant the door of the room Leila was in," Chelby added.

"Oh my God," Shyla whispered.

"Yeah, I know, it's crazy, and I don't know what to do," Chelby admitted.

"What the heck are you talking about? You gotta tell the cops!" Shyla shouted.

"Shhhh, not so loud, remember you're not supposed to know this," Chelby reminded. Shyla calmed back down, remembering that Chelby's parents weren't too far from Chelby's room.

"My fault, my fault, but you gotta go tell the cops," Shyla replied.

"I know, but tell them what, that I read Ms. Kaylie's mind, and that I know where the little girl is?" Chelby asked.

"Yes, duh!" Shyla responded, gently smacking Chelby on the forehead.

"Ok, but then what? I'm in a straight jacket in some hospital or some science lab with tubes in me somewhere. No way! Has to be another way," Chelby responded.

"Oh yeah, you're right. I didn't think that far into it. I wasn't thinking. You have a point," Shyla replied, now smacking herself on the forehead. "So, what we gonna do, cause, we have to do something!"

"Ok, girls, y'all ready?!" Marcus yelled from the living room.

"Ok, Dad, we're coming right now!" Chelby said, hopping off her bed. Shyla gathered her things and hugged Mia before heading to the door to leave.

"Dad, I'm gonna go take that ride with y'all too. Is that ok?" Chelby asked.

"Yeah, that's cool, but let's go now," Marcus instructed.

"Thank you again for dinner, Mrs. Williams. It was delicious!" Shyla admitted.

"Sure, anytime. I made a plate for your mother as well," Mia mentioned, handing a wrapped plate to Shyla on her way out.

"Oh, thank you, my mother is going to love it, I'm sure. Have a good night," Shyla said.

"I hope your mother does, and you're very welcome. Goodnight, sweetie," Mia responded. Marcus, Chelby, and Shyla headed out the door to Marcus' car to bring Shyla home for the night.

Once in the car, Marcus turned the volume up on his radio, which was perfect for Chelby and Shyla to continue their conversation without being heard. Shyla was still having a tough time digesting all of what Chelby was feeding her. Not so much because of doubt, but more so in amazement.

"This is it, right?" Marcus asked, pulling in front of Shyla's house.

"Yes, Mr. Williams, thank you," Shyla replied.

"You're welcome, Shyla. Come by anytime. Oh, and tell your mother I said hello," Marcus responded.

"I will," Shyla said, waving goodnight to Marcus. Chelby got out of the car to walk Shyla to her door.

"Remember Shyla, not a word to anybody," Chelby instructed, holding her fist to Shyla's chin.

"I know, girl, I know, I got you, I promise," Shyla replied. The two gave one another a hug goodnight as Marcus watched, smiling from outside his car door.

Marcus made sure Shyla was in the house safe before departing to go back home. "I like Shyla, such a sweet and cute little girl. A little crazy, but sweet," Marcus noted while laughing.

"Yeah, I like her too," Chelby replied.

"I know you do, baby, I can tell. Y'all two couldn't stop whispering back there on the ride here. I wasn't listening, but man," Marcus mentioned.

"Um, Dad, about that, I kinda have something to tell you," Chelby mumbled.

"What's wrong?" Marcus asked, looking at Chelby's face through the rearview mirror.

"I, um, kinda told Shyla bout the things I can do," Chelby admitted.

"What you mean, the things you could do?" Marcus asked with a stern voice.

"You know, about my abilities, Dad," Chelby responded.

"What?!" Marcus shouted, swerving into another lane and abruptly going back into the lane he was in prior. "Are you serious? What in the world were you thinking?!" he yelled. "Give me a second," Marcus said as he got closer to the apartment.

Marcus soon found parking in front of their apartment but wanted to finish the conversation before going inside. "Chelby, are you crazy? What did I tell you? Nobody can know about this. That means not anybody!" Marcus exclaimed, raising his voice.

"Dad, I know, but I trust her. She's really a great friend to me," Chelby responded.

"Chelby, that's not the point, and Shyla is not the issue here. It's about who she may tell and what they may do with that information once receiving it. This is very serious. You need to listen when I tell you something concerning your safety. You have a lot of evil and crazy people out there in this world, and I have to make sure I protect you from those kinds of people by any means, even if you don't like it," Marcus explained.

Chelby sighed but didn't say a thing. "Listen, let's just go upstairs and talk about it with your mother," Marcus said, getting out of his car.

"Uh-huh," Chelby mumbled, getting out of the car as well.

"It's ok. Everything will be alright ," Marcus said, putting his arm around Chelby.

Once they both went upstairs, Chelby told her mother what she and Shyla discussed in her room. Chelby explained how much this secret had been weighing on her and that she wasn't intentionally going against what they told her not to do. Mia was shockingly not as disappointed as Marcus was.

"You don't seem too bothered by this at all, Amia. Do you understand exactly how serious this is?" Marcus questioned.

"Of course, I do. You know I pray over Chelby constantly and pray about these abilities as well," Mia replied.

"So why is your reaction just so understanding right now," Marcus asked. "Because that's what Chelby needs right now, understanding, not direction. She acknowledged what she did wrong, Chelby understands, but as she said, it's been bothering her a lot," Mia responded.

"Ok, I understand that part, and I agree, but still," Marcus replied.

"Plus, that is her best friend. I mean, they talk all the time, and I think she's a trustworthy friend to Chelby, right?" Mia said as Chelby nodded her head in agreement.

"I just think we need to talk to Shyla together, just to make sure that she fully understands how serious this secret is," Mia explained.

"Alright," Marcus said with hesitation.

"Ok, I'll call or text Ms. Baxter and ask if Shyla can come over for dinner again this weekend, and we'll talk to her then about everything, ok?" Mia said.

"Yes, Mom, that'll be perfect," Chelby replied.

"Yeah, that's cool with me," Marcus responded.

"Ok, Chelby, go get some rest. Back to school tomorrow," Mia instructed.

"Ok, Mom, goodnight. Goodnight, Dad," Chelby said to both Marcus and Mia.

"Ok, baby. Goodnight. Love you," Marcus replied.

"Good night. Love you too," Mia responded. Not too long after Chelby went to bed, Mia and Marcus went to bed as well.

Chapter 8

The Rescue

The following day at school, Chelby still had so many things on her mind. On her way to class, she bumped right into a student dropping all of his books out of his hand.

"Hey, you didn't see me?" the boy asked, throwing his hands up in the air.

"Oh, I'm so, so, sorry about that," Chelby replied, bending over to pick the books up off of the floor. After realizing that it was only an accident, the boy crouched down to help Chelby pick up the books. "Don't worry about it. It was a mistake," the boy said as he hurried off to class. Chelby watched the boy run off, wondering how her thoughts may be affecting her more than she had hoped. When she turned to watch the boy walk away, she saw Shyla running towards her.

Shyla leaped at her and shouted, "What's up, Wonder Girl?!"

"Shhh, shhh, be quiet, Shyla! What's wrong with you?" Chelby whispered.

"Girl, ain't nobody heard me or even know what I'm talking about if they did," Shyla replied.

"Man, I knew I should've kept this to myself," Chelby mumbled under her breath.

"Relax, relax, I'm just messing with you. Are you ok?" Shyla asked.

"Yeah, just a lot on my mind, that's all," Chelby admitted.

"Oh, ok, I understand, but listen, at lunch, I want to talk to you about something, to see what you think," Shyla stated.

"Oh, ok," Chelby replied as she walked into class, followed right behind by Shyla.

At lunch, the two sat down at the end of one of the lunch tables. As they started to eat, Chelby whispered to Shyla, "So what did you have to ask me? What did you want to talk about?" Shyla looked around the cafeteria, then looked on both sides of her to make sure no one was listening. "Ok, so don't freak out," Shyla said.

"Don't freak out? Obviously, if you tell me not to freak out, I'm gonna freak out," Chelby responded.

"Ok, so last night, I had a quick talk with my mother..." Shyla began.

Chelby cut her off and said, "No, no, no! Please tell me you didn't tell your mother. Please tell me you didn't!"

"No, of course not, Chelby. I already told you your secret is good with me," Shyla replied.

"So, what was this talk about?" Chelby questioned. "I was getting to that. So, you know my mother knows Ms. Kaylie, right?" Shyla asked.

"No, I didn't know... She knows her how, though?" Chelby questioned.

"I'm about to tell you. So long story short, my mother knew her from back in the day before she started driving the ice-cream truck. They weren't friends like that, but she knew her from around the way. Anyway, she said that Ms. Kaylie had a young child, a girl, but she drowned in a pool when she was about five or six. She said that nobody spoke of what happened to the girl with Ms. Kaylie 'cause they knew it was too painful," Shyla explained.

"Wow, that's so sad," Chelby replied.

"Yeah, I know, my mother said that's why she thinks she took the job to drive the ice-cream truck, to be closer to kids. I guess she still misses her daughter," Shyla added.

"Yeah, I can understand that," Chelby replied.

Shyla stopped to look around the cafeteria again. Luckily no one was paying attention to either one of them. "Ok, but that's not it. My mother told me that she lives close to my house. I asked her where, and she told me, and she's right, not too far from me at all. I know the area well," Shyla mentioned.

"O....K..., so what, you know where she lives, what does that have to do with anything, Shyla?" Chelby asked.

"This girl's brain doesn't work," Shyla responded, rubbing her forehead.

"I'm saying we can take a bus to where Ms. Kaylie lives. You do your Avenger thing, sneak in, and save that little girl!" Shyla exclaimed.

"What, are you nuts?!" Chelby questioned.

"Look, I know where she lives. I'll go with you. We can be like Batgirl and um, Robin-nette!" Shyla assured. Chelby looked confused.

"Who in the world is Robin-nette?" Chelby asked.

"Man, I don't know, her sidekick, I guess. Or Wonder Woman and um..." Shyla said, thinking.

"Oh, I know, I can be Black Widow, yeah, that's me!" Shyla announced.

"Black Widow? So, you know how to shoot a bow and arrow now, is that what you're telling me?" Chelby teased.

"Hey, well, I can throw rocks!" Shyla replied.

Chelby looked down at the table, shaking her head from side to side.

"But seriously, we need to do something. We need to go save that girl," Shyla insisted.

"We have to think this out first. We can't just go up in Ms. Kaylie's house and say, hey, give us the little girl or else!" Chelby responded.

"Oh my God!" Shyla put her hand over her face then shook her head. "We'll go right after school while Ms. Kaylie is making her rounds. You sneak in while I watch to see if she's coming," Shyla explained.

"How am I supposed to do that? I don't have a key?" Chelby questioned.

"A key? Aren't you Wonder Girl or something?" Shyla asked.

"Stop saying that!" Chelby mumbled, grinding her teeth.

"I'm just saying, use your abilities. How else would we get in?" Shyla asked. Chelby rolled her eyes and sighed. "Look, Chelby, I know you've been thinking about a way to do this. Now we have a way, so we have to!" Shyla exclaimed.

Chelby took a deep breath before admitting, "I'm just scared, that's all."

"Chelby, I'm scared too, but guess what, how do you think that little girl is feeling right now? Haven't been home in weeks, haven't seen her family, don't know if she'll see them again, that's too scary," Shyla replied.

"Yeah, you're right, you're right. So, after school?" Chelby asked.

"Yeah, right after school, so the sun will still be up. Meet me right in front," Shyla replied.

"Alright," Chelby agreed. Not too long after Chelby said alright, lunch came to an end, and the students having lunch were instructed to head back to class. Chelby went back to class with thoughts of not following through with Shyla's plan. Her palms were moist with sweat from nervousness and anxiety.

Once school ended, before meeting Shyla outside in the front, Chelby rushed to the bathroom to throw water on her face. She dried off, looked in the mirror, and said a quick prayer that both she and Shyla got back home safe at the end of this. She took a deep breath and walked out of the bathroom to meet Shyla in front of the school.

"You good girl?" Shyla asked as Chelby approached her.

"Yeah, just nervous, but I'm ok," Chelby admitted. The girls walked to the bus stop to take the bus to Ms. Kaylie's house.

"Hey, Shyla, let me borrow your phone real quick so I can text my mother to tell her I'll be at the shop a little late today," Chelby requested.

"Of course," Shyla responded, handing the phone to Chelby. Once the bus arrived, both girls got on. At each stop that the girls came to while on the bus, Chelby struggled with the feeling to get off and go home, but young little Leila would pop up in her mind. So Chelby forced herself to be brave and continued on to Ms. Kaylie's house, tucking away her fear for the greater purpose. "Hey Chelby, couple more stops, then we have to walk about a block or two once we get off, ok?" Shyla mentioned.

"Ok, cool," Chelby replied, pretending to be braver than how she felt. A few stops came and went as Chelby stared out the window.

"Next stop," Shyla whispered. Chelby responded with a head nod. Chelby's heart was starting to beat faster as they approached the next stop. Her clammy hand gripped the top of the seat in front of her as she got up.

Once Chelby and Shyla got off, they walked the long block to Ms. Kaylie's house. It seemed to take forever for both nervous girls.

"I think this is...yeah, this is it," Shyla said. The house was a big yellow old fashion looking place. There was a silver gate in front of the steps leading towards the front door. Inside of the gate, we're small green bushes trimmed and shaped nicely, making a path to the door.

"Ok, so now what?" Chelby asked.

"Let's look around first to make sure Ms. Kaylie isn't home," Shyla responded. And both girls did just that. The house didn't have much of a backyard, but on the side of the house was a driveway leading to an old garage, and the garage door was left half-open.

"Doesn't look like anybody's home," Chelby mentioned, checking out the side of the house.

"Yeah, no cars here either, so that's good," Shyla replied, looking into the garage from a distance. The girls continued to look around, looking up into windows, just to make sure they were right about no one being home at the time.

"Nah, nobody's here," Chelby said.

"Ok, perfect, Chelby, get in there and do your thing, then," Shyla responded. Chelby felt a lump come in her throat as she approached the door, more nervous than she's ever been.

"Wonder Girl, do your thing," Shyla whispered.

"I don't know if I can do this, Shyla," Chelby whimpered, looking as if she wanted to cry from fear of the unknown. Shyla walked up to her, looking up at Chelby into her eyes and placing a hand on top of each of Chelby's shoulders. She gripped both shoulders and let out a sigh.

"Look, Chelby, I'm right here with you. If that little girl is in there, we have to help her, and we have to be brave for her. She needs you. You can do this!" Shyla assured.

Chelby briefly closed her eyes before reopening them again. She looked at Shyla as she felt a warm sensation going throughout her body. She took a deep breath, then nodded at Shyla.

"Ok," Chelby responded.

Shyla smiled and replied, "I'll stay right here as a lookout."

"Ok," Chelby said as she turned away from Shyla, heading towards the front door.

"Go get 'em, Wonder Girl!" Shyla whispered, tapping Chelby's butt with the back of her hand for motivation. Chelby stopped, shook her head twice, but didn't look back, continuing towards the door. Shyla stood outside the gate, checking each car that passed by.

Once Chelby was at the door, she tried to open it quietly by turning the doorknob back and forth.

"It's locked," Chelby whispered.

"No, really? Duh, of course, it's locked. Do your ability thing, girl. Can't you just disappear and walk through the door" Shyla whispered.

A woman walked by the house, staring at the girls as she walked by. "Afternoon, ma'am," Shyla said waving, as the woman passed. The woman didn't respond but looked away once Shyla acknowledged her. "Whew," Shyla murmured.

"It doesn't work like that Shyla, I can't just walk-through walls," Chelby responded.

"Girl, do something. We cannot be out here looking crazy all day. Think of something," Shyla replied.

Chelby turned back to the door and gripped the doorknob tight as she rammed her shoulder into the door. But nothing happened. She paused and tried it again, with more force, this time, but once again, nothing happened. Chelby released the tight grip she had around the doorknob.

Shyla looked on, shaking her head in disbelief. Chelby closed her eyes and became real still. Shyla turned back around, paying close attention to the passing cars and people in the area. Chelby began to concentrate. Her forearm started to itch as she opened her eyes again. She was able to see her reflection through one of the door's glass panes. Knowing her task at hand helped her focus.

She tightly gripped the doorknob again, slamming her shoulder into the door for the third time, but this time, it worked. She broke the locks of the door, and the door slowly opened.

"I did it," Chelby whispered to Shyla.

"Whoa," Shyla replied. Shyla left where she was standing and walked up to the door with Chelby. They both walked in with apprehension, not knowing where to move next. On the main floor, there were two doors. One looked like a closet, and the other looked like it led to a bedroom. There was also a stairwell leading up to the second floor of the house. Shyla pointed to the second floor.

"You hear that?" Shyla asked in a low tone.

"Yeah, I do," Chelby answered. They both could hear a TV on upstairs, with sounds of cartoons playing on it.

"You go, and I'll check around here," Shyla instructed.

"Ok," Chelby whispered. Shyla checked the door that looked like it led to a bedroom, but it was locked. Chelby made her way up the stairs towards the noise of the TV. Once upstairs, she noticed three doors. Two of the doors were slightly opened, and one was closed shut.

As Chelby slowly made her way towards the rooms, she abruptly stopped because of the floor creaking underneath her feet. Once realizing the nature of the sound, she continued. As she approached, the first room on her right was a room filled with pink and lavender. In that room was a small bed that had pink sheets neatly tucked into it. The paint on the walls was lavender. A small table and chair were next to the bed, which were also pink, matching the room's theme. A small toy kitchen set was directly under pictures drawn by a child. Above that, in the center of the room, was a picture in a frame. It was of a younger Ms. Kaylie holding a little girl on her lap, with matching outfits.

Chelby gasped when seeing the picture but continued to the room where she heard the cartoon sounds. The second room she came to on her left had dim lighting and something that made her feel like her heart may drop right out of her chest. A man was sleeping soundly in bed. Chelby anxiously thought to run back downstairs and out of the house, but she intended to find the little girl. She slowly and lightly crept to the last room, which was facing her. She tried to open the door, but it was locked closed. She also noticed a thick padlock attached to the door as well.

Chelby put her ear to the door, hoping to hear something distinctive, but she could only make out the noise from the TV. Suddenly, the man in the other room was drawn to Chelby's attention as she heard him making sounds while rolling over in his bed. Chelby took a deep breath to relax, but mainly to focus. The lights in the house began to flicker, then stop. Her forearm started to itch again. Her feet and legs began to disappear, followed by her torso, arms, and hands, with, lastly, her head becoming completely invisible. Chelby walked back to the room with the man sleeping and walked in. She was in search of the key to the padlock.

She quietly moved around the room, looking for the key, but initially, she had no such luck. Chelby thought to herself if she busted through the locked door, the man surely would wake up.

She continued to search but couldn't find any keys. As she made her way out of the room, she saw a coat hanging on the inside of the door. She went to the coat and checked the first pocket she noticed, and there were keys stuffed inside. Chelby slowly and carefully took the keys from the coat pocket that was hanging on the door.

Just then, the man turned over and looked around as he wiped his eyes. Chelby stood still, trying to breathe as lightly as possible. The man looked at his phone and laid back down. Chelby waited for a minute, then made her way back to the locked room. She eagerly went through the keys and found the small key to the padlock.

Once the door was unlocked and she took the padlock off, Chelby had to find access to the door with the knowledge of time not being on her side. Chelby went through several keys before finding the right one. She gently opened the door, trying her best not to wake the man up only a few feet away from her.

As soon as the door opened, she saw the TV that she and Shyla heard from downstairs. Although the TV didn't draw her initial attention once opening the door, Chelby's focus was brought to a bed, which Leila laid tied to and restrained. The missing little girl was lying helplessly, right before Chelby's eyes. Leila groggily moved from side to side, moaning, half-awake, and uncomfortable. Chelby didn't hesitate. She moved over to the knots that tied Leila's legs and arms to the bed, untying the knots and freeing her. She sat Leila up and hugged her. Chelby's face, arms, and hands were seen by Leila first, followed by Chelby's stomach, legs, then feet.

"I'm here to save you, Leila," Chelby whispered.

"Are you an Angel?" Leila asked but then passed right out soon after.

After Leila was completely freed, Chelby picked her up to carry her out. She focused again, slowly becoming invisible, which in turn made Leila invisible as well. Chelby could hear Shyla whispering from downstairs, trying to get her attention.

"Psst! Psst! Chelby, are you ok up there?" Shyla whispered. Chelby tried to hurry to the stairs. "Chelby, where you at? Are you ok?" Shyla called, but Chelby didn't respond. "Chelby, are you good!?" Shyla shouted. Exactly what Chelby was hoping not to happen, did.

The man jumped out of bed and darted out to the stairs. "What, who are you, and how did you get in here?" the man asked. Shyla walked uneasily backward towards the front door.

Shyla shouted again, "Chelby!"

The man turned around and looked at the room where Leila was locked in and noticed that the door was wide open. "Leila?!" the man mumbled, running towards the room. Leila suddenly woke up, startled, and screamed, turning the man's attention to the front of the stairs. Chelby put Leila down, making her visible once again. Then Chelby became clear to see once again as well.

"What in the world?" the man said, watching both Leila and Chelby reappear.

"Leave her alone!" Chelby demanded.

The man quickly reacted and rushed both Chelby and Leila. Chelby clenched her fist tight. He tried to grab Chelby, but Chelby grabbed him, then pushed him down the stairs. Everything seemed to stop for a moment. Chelby picked up Leila and took her downstairs, stepping over the moaning man in the process. Shyla's mouth didn't close until they were all outside the gate.

Shyla wiped Leila's face as Leila hung onto Chelby's neck. "Hey, is that your mother across the street? Wait, is that my mother too?" Shyla asked. Shyla began to squint, trying to make out the woman alongside Chelby's mother.

"Yeah, it is. I texted my mother earlier when you gave me your phone. She must have called your mother to find out exactly where we were," Chelby admitted.

Sirens were heard wailing from down the block. "Here, get Leila. I'm not feeling so good," Chelby said.

"Chelby, what's wrong?" Shyla asked. Chelby went down on one knee as she held herself from falling completely over by holding onto the gate in front of her.

Both mothers, Mrs. Williams and Ms. Baxter ran across the street, ignoring traffic to get to their girls. As they ran up to Chelby and Shyla, the man that was still in the house started to get up from the floor. People that were passing by now stopped to see what was going on as police approached. Whispers throughout the block were drowned out by the raging sirens approaching the scene. Ms. Baxter grabbed Shyla and Leila to bring them away from the house. Mia helped a weak Chelby to her feet and gingerly walked her to where the other ladies were standing.

Dozens of police officers arrived on the scene, and someone must have called the local news because they showed up at the house as well. Once the officers got out their cars, they ordered the man to turn around and get on his knees. After the man complied, a few officers rushed towards him to handcuff the man and stood him up on his feet. The man turned to the crowd ducking his head down into his chest, trying not to be seen by all.

Right before an ambulance was going to take Leila to the hospital for health risk precautions, Mia asked one of the EMTs if they could take a look at Chelby as well. The EMT told Mia that Chelby should also go to the hospital for further observation. Mia agreed and asked Ms. Baxter and Shyla to follow the ambulances to the hospital.

On the way into the ambulance, Chelby, and the man from Ms. Kaylie's house, made eye contact with one another, and a frightening look came across his face. "Demon, she's a demon! I saw her appear with Leila out of thin air! She's the devil, I tell you!" the man frantically shouted.

"Yeah, yeah, get in the car," one of the officers said as he shoved the man in the back of the police car. As Chelby stared off into the crowd and before getting up into the ambulance, she recognized someone else in the back seat of the police car. It was Ms. Kaylie, with her face soaked with tears. Shyla shook her head in disgust as Chelby looked on with empathy.

I can't believe she took that little girl, Mia thought, as she held on to Chelby's hand.

"Yeah, I know Mom, me either," Chelby said.

Chapter 9

Gift or Curse?

As the cops, ambulance, and local news roared through traffic to get to the hospital, all Chelby could think of is why. *Why would Ms. Kaylie do such a horrible thing?*

"I feel like I have the flu again, Mom, like chills this time, too," Chelby explained.

"We are almost there, baby," Mia replied.

Chelby began to sweat, and her throat felt like sandpaper.

"I'm just so happy we got Leila back. How do you think she's doing?" Chelby asked.

"She's probably sound asleep, we'll see her later once we get to the hospital, but I'm glad she's ok as well," Mia responded. "Right now, I'm worried about you."

"I'll be ok, just really weak right now, and my throat is feeling kind of scratchy," Chelby replied.

Once reaching the hospital, Chelby had no energy at all. A nurse took her to one of the emergency rooms in a wheelchair because of her inability to walk at that time. Shyla and Ms. Baxter reached the hospital only minutes after Mia and Chelby did. Unable to go into the room with Chelby at the time, Ms. Baxter and Shyla waited in the waiting area for information on Chelby. The hospital refused to allow the news reporters inside the E.R., so the reporters stayed outside waiting for comments from anybody involved in the day's events.

About a half-hour had passed when Shyla noticed that a man and woman walked straight into Leila's room. "I think those are her parents, Mom," Shyla mentioned, pointing to the couple.

"Yeah, I think you're right. I think they are, Shyla," Ms. Baxter replied.

Just then, Marcus frantically ran into the waiting room with his face full of sweat. "Shyla, are you ok? Where's Chelby?" Marcus asked, trying to catch his breath.

"She's in that room with your wife, Mr. Williams," Ms. Baxter replied.

Marcus ran over to Ms. Baxter and Shyla to hug them both. "Oh, I'm so sorry, Ms. Baxter, how are you? Are you ok?" Marcus asked.

"Don't worry, I fully understand, it's ok, go see your girls. They're in that room right there," Ms. Baxter replied, pointing to the room Mia and Chelby were in.

"Thank you, I'll be right back," Marcus responded, hustling to the room in haste.

"Hey, Mr. Williams, please tell Chelby we are right outside if she needs us. Thank you," Shyla mentioned.

"I definitely will, I promise," Marcus replied, right before he walked in.

As soon as Marcus walked in, he saw Mia standing over Chelby, who was propped up in the hospital bed. They embraced one another but abruptly turned their focus onto Chelby. Marcus noticed that Chelby was hooked up to an I.V., which made him very uncomfortable. He took a glance around the room and let out a sigh as he rubbed the middle of Mia's back, attempting to comfort her.

The nurses coming in and out of the room, the ongoing sounds of the room's equipment, and the many fluorescent lights surrounding them, gave Marcus an unsettling deja vu feeling that he hoped he'd never feel again.

As both worrisome parents watched over Chelby, the doctor walked in. "Mr. And Mrs. Williams, I would say it's great to see you again, but unfortunately, definitely not under these circumstances," Dr. Miller said.

"Dr. Miller, how are you?" Mia asked.

"Yeah, I didn't want to meet like this again," Marcus replied, shaking Dr. Miller's hand. "What's the I.V. for Doc? What's wrong with her?" Marcus asked.

"Yeah, I know parents, I know. So, the I.V. is for her extreme dehydration. Did she have the flu or something? You know it's common this time of year?" Dr. Miller asked. "Um, no, she wasn't sick at all," Marcus responded.

"Was she throwing up a lot, food poisoning?" Dr. Miller questioned. Both Marcus and Mia looked at one another before answering.

"No, I don't think so. She was fine when she left home," Mia replied.

Dr. Miller began to scratch his head as he picked up the chart to look it over, picking up his eyes to the monitors every so often as well. "Wow, very strange then," Dr. Miller responded as he flipped through one of the pages of the chart on Chelby. "But then again, dealing with your special Chelby here, nothing should surprise me," Dr. Miller mentioned with a slight grin.

"Is she going to be alright," Marcus asked.

"Yes, she'll be fine, she just needs the proper hydration, and she'll be good to go," Dr. Miller replied.

"Thank God," Mia said, holding Marcus' arm and rubbing Chelby's hand at the same time.

Chelby had sat up some, while still in bed, to drink some of the water a nurse had left for her on the overbed table. "How are you feeling, baby girl?" Marcus asked.

"Not too bad, Dad, just a little out of it, that's all," Chelby responded. Marcus leaned in close to Chelby so he wouldn't have to speak too loudly.

"Good, cause I'm a kill you! You'll already be in the hospital, so they can try and save you after," Marcus whispered.

"Dad?!" Chelby murmured.

"Don't '*Dad*' me. What in God's name were you and your little sidekick thinking? You know how dangerous and unsafe that was? How dumb of a decision that was? You both could have been seriously hurt, or worse!" Marcus scolded.

Chelby looked at her father without replying, understanding how wrong and unsafe her actions of going to Ms. Kaylie's house alone with Shyla were.

"By the way, Shyla and her mother are outside waiting to see you too. Forgot to tell you that," Marcus mentioned.

"Oh, she is?" Chelby eagerly asked.

"Listen, forget about that right now. What transpired today could have drastically gone a different way. Do you understand what I'm telling you, girl?" Marcus whispered.

Mia bumped Marcus in his side to stop him from scolding Chelby. "Not now, Marcus. Let's go outside for a second and let Chelby see her friend real quick," Mia said.

"Yeah, alright," Marcus responded. They both went outside the room, and Mia signaled for Shyla to go in.

"You can go in, Shyla, if you want to see Chelby real quick," Mia told Shyla.

"Yes, I do. Can I go right now?" Shyla asked. Mia nodded her head yes.

"Hey Ma, I'll be right back," Shyla said.

"Thank you, Mrs. Williams," Shyla replied.

"No problem, Shyla, we'll be out here waiting with your mother," Mia responded. "Don't be too long, Shyla," Ms. Baxter mentioned. Shyla walked in with a nervous smile on her face. She was observing everything going on in the room, as well as the I.V. that was connected to Chelby. Shyla's eyes grew big as she approached the hospital bed.

"Dang, what's all of this?" Shyla questioned as she continued to look around the room. Chelby sat up higher in the hospital bed to talk with Shyla.

"Thank you so much for coming to the hospital for me, and please thank your mother for me when you go back outside, too," Chelby responded.

"Of course, no need, girl. Told you before, we're in this together," Shyla replied. Chelby tried to sit up even further to hug Shyla but could not because of the I.V. still in her arm.

"Man, what's this thing hooked up to you?" Shyla asked.

"Oh, that's called an I.V.... It's supposed to help rehydrate me," Chelby replied.

"Oh, I didn't know," Shyla mumbled. "Is it working, though? Are you feeling any better?"

"Yeah, actually, I do. Starting to feel much better than before," Chelby admitted.

"Yeah, I didn't know what was wrong with you out there. All of a sudden, you just fell to your knees," Shyla mentioned. "I know, I just started to feel so out of it," Chelby replied.

"But girl, you did it. You got Leila back," Shyla whispered. "No, we got her back, Robinette!" Chelby whispered, with a smirk on her face.

"Oh, snap! Don't be telling people my alter ego up in here, girl! You gotta keep that on the low," Shyla responded, smiling back at Chelby.

"You know, I saw what you did upstairs in Ms. Kaylie's house, right? That was amazing!" Shyla whispered.

"I know you saw," Chelby replied.

"How did you make Leila disappear too," Shyla asked.

"Shh, I think it's 'cause I was holding her, but yeah, I know you saw everything," Chelby responded.

"Whoever that man was in Ms. Kaylie's house, you know, he saw everything too, right?" Shyla asked.

Chelby let out a deep sigh. "Yeah, I know he did. He was calling me a demon when we were outside," Chelby responded. "Yeah, I know, I heard that too. I'd probably think the same thing if I didn't know you were really Wonder Girl," Shyla joked.

"Shyla, how many times I gotta tell you about that?" Chelby whispered, grinding her teeth together.

"My fault, my fault, just saying," Shyla replied. Mia walked in as Chelby and Shyla continued talking.

"Hey Shyla, go back outside for a second, please. The doctor has to check on your friend," Mia instructed.

"Ok, no problem, Ms. Mia. I'll see you outside, Chelby," Shyla replied, waving.

Soon as Shyla walked back out, Dr. Miller, along with Marcus and Mia, came back into the room. "So how are we feeling, Ms. Chelby, doing any better?" Dr. Miller asked.

"Much better, Dr. Miller. I'm feeling so much better than before," Chelby responded.

"Oh, much better, huh? That's great! So let me get one of the nurses to take this I.V. out, and you'll be good to go. How does that sound?" Dr. Miller asked.

"Sounds good to me!" Chelby responded. "Ok great, do you have any questions for me?" Dr. Miller asked.

"No, I don't. I'm fine, thank you," Chelby replied.

"Ok great, let me talk to your parents for a second, and I'll be right outside if you need anything," Dr. Miller said.

"Ok, thank you so much," Chelby responded. Dr. Miller pulled both Mia and Marcus over to the side.

"She's looking much better now. But continue to watch her and keep her hydrated. Pedialyte or Gatorade will do the trick if she needs it. Other than that, you are good to go," Dr. Miller concluded.

"Thank you, Doctor," Mia said. Marcus shook Dr. Miller's hand as the doctor left the room.

"So, listen, we'll be right outside, ok?" Marcus said. "Ok, cool," Chelby replied.

Once the I.V. was taken out of her arm, Chelby got her things together to leave. She heard a knock at the door, then Dr. Miller walked in. "Excuse me, Chelby, you have someone out there that wants to speak with you," he said.

"Wants to speak to me? Ok, tell them I'm coming out right now," Chelby responded. Chelby got her things together and walked out of the hospital room. Once outside the room, the first person she noticed was little Leila standing in the middle of her parents with a smile that warmed her heart.

"How are you? I'm Mr. Barrett, and this is Mrs. Barrett. We are Leila's parents. Are you the one who saved our little princess?" Mr. Barrett asked, with tears slowly rolling down his cheeks. Chelby just smiled without answering. "God bless you. Can we hug you?"

Mr. Barrett asked, looking at Chelby's father for approval. Marcus nodded his head, yes.

Soon as both Mr. and Mrs. Barrett hugged Chelby, they both burst out crying. "Thank you. We can never repay you for this," Mr. Barrett said, still clutching Chelby tightly. Mrs. Barrett was crying too much to form the words needed to show her undying appreciation.

As the Barrett's let go of their embrace around Chelby, Mrs. Barrett looked at Chelby as she struggled to talk. "How did you do this all by yourself?" Mrs. Barrett asked.

"Uh-Um," Shyla gestured, acting as if she was clearing her throat.

"Well, I wasn't by myself. My friend right here, Shyla, was right there with me.

The Barrett's gave Shyla a long embrace as well. "So, girls, how did you do this? How were you able to find and save our little girl?" Mrs. Barrett curiously asked.

Both Chelby and Shyla turned to look at one another. "Well....um..." Shyla mumbled.

Before she could answer, just then, two officers walked out of the elevator towards

Mr. and Mrs. Williams, Ms. Baxter, Shyla, and the Barrett family. "Mr. and Mrs. Williams, Ms. Baxter, we have a few questions to ask your daughters at this time. I'm officer Hernandez, and this is officer Moore. We want to ask just a few basic questions about what exactly transpired a few hours ago and how they were able to rescue Leila. If you don't mind, of course," officer Hernandez asked.

A concerned look came across both Shyla and Chelby's faces, not knowing exactly how to explain what took place a short time ago to the officers or anybody else for that matter.

"So, ladies, did any of you know the woman and or man that was living in the house that you rescued Leila from?" Officer Hernandez asked.

Both Shyla and Chelby looked at one another, but only Shyla spoke. "Yes, we, we know, Ms. Kaylie," Shyla stuttered to answer.

Officer Moore wrote what Shyla said down on a small notepad as Officer Hernandez asked another question. "Oh, so you *do* know her. How do you know Ms. Kaylie?" Officer Hernandez asked.

"She's the ice cream lady. She's the neighborhood ice-cream lady," Shyla replied. Officer Moore continued to jot things down.

"Oh, ok. That's right, she is. So, what brought you to her house today, and how did you get inside without Ms. Kaylie, the ice-cream lady, there?" Officer Hernandez asked.

Both Chelby and Shyla looked at one another again, but this time Chelby spoke. "Um, well..." Chelby said as Marcus cut her off.

"Listen, Officers, both these girls had a trying day, plus my daughter is not feeling well, and they both could use some rest. Can we please do this another day?" Marcus asked.

Both officers looked at one another, then back at the families. "Sure, yes, we understand, Mr. Williams, and I agree, we'll do this another time. Take your girls home to get some rest. But some things need to be answered, Mr. Williams, so we will be in contact with you," Officer Hernandez said.

"Have a good night," Officer Moore replied as he closed his notepad.

"I understand, sir, and thank you for your consideration," Mr. Williams responded. As the families hugged one another goodnight, Marcus stopped the officers before they left.

"Excuse me, Officers, is the press still downstairs?" Marcus asked.

"Yes, I believe that they are. Is that a problem?" Officer Hernandez replied.

"Yes, it is sir, I don't want the girl's names or faces on the news, if possible," Marcus responded.

"Oh, I see. I can understand that. I wouldn't want my kids on the news either," Officer Hernandez replied. "So, we'll go out the back way to avoid the press and cameras. Ok, Mr. Williams?"

"Oh, that's perfect," Marcus replied. As the officers led the Williams family along with Shyla and her mother down the back staircase, one of the officers stopped to ask a question.

"So, where did you park?" Officer Moore asked.

"We all parked near the front entrance of the ER," Marcus replied.

"Ok, so we'll stay with the girls. You go get your cars and bring it to the back for the young ladies," Officer Moore said.

"Ok, got it. And thank you, once again," Marcus responded.

"Not a problem, Mr. Williams," the officers replied.

Everybody did just as planned, as the Barrett family, now complete with Leila, went through the front entrance facing the press on their way out. Marcus had Shyla and Chelby with him as Mia rode home with Ms. Baxter.

"Hey Dad, can you stop real quick to get something to eat?" Chelby asked.

"Yeah, it is late, so what would you like?" Marcus asked.

"I feel like some nuggets and fries. Can you stop at Mickey D's, please?" Chelby asked.

"Ok, cool, do you want anything, Shyla?" Marcus asked.

"Yes, please, a cheeseburger and fries are good, and maybe a sprite, thank you," Shyla replied.

"Ok, no problem, let me just text your mother to let her know that we are making a brief stop," Marcus responded.

On the way to McDonald's, the girls whispered back and forth about the long, eventful day they just had. Marcus tried to be nosey but only heard bits in pieces of their conversation.

After ordering and picking up the food, they headed to Shyla's house to drop her off.

"Listen, girls, about tonight, please, please, don't ever do anything like that again without letting me or your mother know what you are planning to do," Marcus instructed.

"I did text Mom to tell her where we were, Dad, but I understand what you mean," Chelby replied.

"Yes, we understand, Mr. Williams. You should have seen Wonder Girl go, though!" Shyla mentioned. Marcus smiled without the girls knowing.

"Wonder Girl, huh?" Marcus asked.

"Shyla!" Chelby shouted, grinding her teeth.

"That's a cute name," Marcus said.

"See, I told you," Shyla responded.

"Look, that's not my name, and that's not me. This is just too much. I'm too young for all of this," Chelby replied.

"I know what you are saying, baby girl, but let me tell you a story," Marcus responded.

"Dad!?" Chelby murmured.

"No, a quick story, I promise," Marcus answered.

"So, when I was a boy, I had this favorite cartoon I used to watch," Marcus said before Shyla interrupted him.

"Wait, there were TV's around when you were a boy?" Shyla questioned.

"Shyla, how old do you think I am?" Marcus asked.

"I don't know, ancient?" Shyla replied. Marcus gave out a sigh.

"So anyway, yes, there were TV's around, and this cartoon, one of my favorite cartoons growing up, was called the Thundercats," Marcus admitted.

"Thundercats?!" both Chelby and Shyla replied.

"Just listen, I'm getting to my point!" Marcus continued. "So, there were these cat slash humans that came from another planet to Earth, which in this show was called Third Earth. So, the leader was named Lion-O. He was chosen to be the leader once he came of age. Now here's the thing, on the way to earth, on the spaceship they were on, the boy Lion-o turned into a man by some malfunction of the ship, but he hadn't truly aged in years, just in the body," Marcus continued.

"Dad, I thought this was gonna be quick," Chelby said.

"Just listen! So, he had to lead his people and protect them, all this responsibility, all as a boy in a man's body. You get what I'm trying to say?" Marcus asked.

"No, Dad, I don't," Chelby replied.

"Yeah, Mr. Williams, you lost me," Shyla responded.

"So, the point is, Lion-O, like you, have been giving abilities and responsibilities at a very young age, but it's because you were chosen for this. Even when things are tough, you have to persevere because people will need you, understand?" Marcus concluded.

"Yes, I guess so, Dad," Chelby replied.

"Um, Mr. Williams," Shyla said. "Yes, Shyla," Marcus responded.

"You could've just said Chelby's Wonder Girl, and she gotta look out for all of us. I'm just saying..." Shyla replied. Marcus sighed.

"Shyla, we are right outside your house, just so you know," Marcus responded with a smirk.

"I was just trying to help, sheesh!" Shyla replied, laughing.

"Yeah, uh-huh, I know you were, have a good night, Shyla, and thank you for being there with Chelby today," Marcus replied.

"Thanks for the food, Mr. Williams, and about Chelby, no problem, I'm her sidekick!" Shyla responded.

"Later, crazy girl, see you tomorrow," Chelby said as Shyla headed to her apartment.

"See you tomorrow, Chelby," Shyla replied, waving back to her.

"That's one crazy friend you got there, Chelby, but a good one," Marcus mentioned.

"Yeah, I know. She's the best!" Chelby replied.

After reaching home, Mia, Marcus, and Chelby watched the news to see what it said about the events earlier that day. They waited and waited, and finally, the Barrett family was on the screen. Leila looked so happy to be back in the arms of her parents, but what they all were honestly waiting for, is if they mentioned Chelby and Shyla. Luckily Leila told the news reporters that an angel had come and saved her, but no mention of either Chelby or Shyla. That night Mia was too tired to do Chelby's hair, so she told Chelby to put it in a ponytail, and she'll do it later that weekend. So Chelby did just that.

Not too long after she laid down, she began to scratch on her forearm. The itching made it more apparent precisely what was happening. The tree-like mark on her forearm began to glow as it did time after time before.

Chelby screamed out, "Dad!" as she rolled out of bed onto her bedroom floor. Both Mia and Marcus got out of bed and ran into Chelby's room to find Chelby hunched over on the floor in discomfort.

"Chelby...Chelby, what's wrong!? "Mia yelled. Chelby didn't answer her mother right away, and she continued to hunch over into a ball for a few more seconds.

"I'm ok, I'm ok," Chelby assured as she stood up.

"What happened? You feel sick again?" Marcus asked.

"No, I'm ok now, Dad. I've felt like this before, you know, whenever Mom would do my hair," Chelby replied.

"What exactly does that feeling feel like?" Marcus asked.

Chelby looked up to the ceiling for a second, gently biting the side of her lip, thinking about the question her father just requested. "Well, it's hard to explain," Chelby responded.

"Try Chelby. I'm curious about how you feel during that time," Marcus said.

"Ok, so, it's a pain, but not exactly pain," Chelby replied.

"Explain, Chelby," Marcus instructed.

"Ok, so, you know when your foot falls asleep, it's like that, but all over like a nagging pain, but not really pain. It's more of the tingly sensation you feel when your foot falls asleep. You kind of understand?" Chelby asked.

"Oh wow, yeah. I do understand," Marcus replied.

"It goes away pretty fast, though. Once the itching on my arm stops, that funny feeling stops too," Chelby explained.

"I wonder what happened this time 'cause I didn't do your hair or use the dryer, but it's as if I did," Mia mentioned.

"I don't know, Mom, but I feel fine now," Chelby replied.

"You sure you don't feel any different than usual, Chelby?" Mia asked.

"Nah, I feel regular, Mom," Chelby replied. Marcus's pocket started to vibrate, then ring.

"Hey guys, one second. This is the police calling," Marcus blurted. Chelby looked nervous, as did Mia. "I'll go in the other room," Marcus whispered.

"Mom, you think everything is ok with Leila?" Chelby asked.

"I hope so, but I'm sure it is. She's back with her parents now, Chelby, so they're a complete family again. To tell you the truth, though, I'm more worried about what the police may want to ask you," Mia responded.

"Yeah, I know, Mom. I don't want to lie, but I'm a little afraid of what may happen if I am forced to tell the truth," Chelby admitted.

"I know, sweetie, but we have to have faith that God will protect us since we are doing the right thing the best way we know how to," Mia explained.

"You're right, Mom. Things will be ok," Chelby assured. Before Chelby and Mia could finish their conversation, Marcus abruptly came back into the room.

"So, what did they have to say, Marcus?" Mia eagerly asked.

"Yeah, Dad, was it bad?" Chelby asked with concern.

"Well, I'll tell you everything he said," Marcus replied. "First thing he mentioned was that Leila was fine after the doctors thoroughly checked her out in the hospital. So that was great news to hear. Secondly, the officer noted that Ms. Kaylie did admit to kidnapping Leila and explained that she was being brought up on charges for that horrific act.

"The officer added that her mental stability we're in question after admitting the reasoning for kidnapping Leila, but he wouldn't divulge that information to me. But lastly, he said that the man at Kaylie's house was her new boyfriend. There was no evidence that he had anything to do with the kidnapping. Ms. Kaylie lied to him and told him that Leila was her child from a previous marriage, so with that said, they have to let him go tonight. One thing that did bother me was that the man brought you up when he was being questioned," Marcus concluded.

"What? Brought Chelby up, how, what did he say?" Mia asked.

"Yeah, what did he say, Dad?" Chelby questioned as well.

"He kept saying that he doesn't know how you got into the house and that you appeared out of thin air, said he saw it with his own eyes," Marcus replied.

"What?!" Mia asked.

"No way!" Chelby said.

"Well, good thing the police laughed it off. He said the man must have still been sleeping or something," Marcus said. Both Mia and Chelby let out a long sigh of relief.

"Well, that's good, baby, as long as they don't harass you over this," Mia told Chelby.

"Yeah, I know, that's true," Chelby replied.

"Listen, it's getting late, baby, you still have school in the morning, but only if you feel up for it, though," Mia said.

"Of course, I do, Mom. I'm good. Ok, Mom, goodnight, love you," Chelby replied.

"Love you too, goodnight," Mia responded.

"Chelby, you're sure you are ok?" Marcus asked.

"Yes, I'm good, Dad, goodnight, love you, Chelby responded.

"Love you too, baby girl, goodnight," Marcus replied. With all three exhausted from the eventful day they just endured, the Williams family went to bed.

The following day in lunch at school, Chelby told Shyla everything the police officer had told her father. She also spoke about Leila, in which Shyla was so happy to hear any good news about the little girl they recently saved. Shyla asked about Ms. Kaylie, but unfortunately, the information and facts weren't too pleasant.

"So how are you feeling today though, all better?" Shyla asked.

"Yeah, I feel good. I forgot to tell you that the thing happened last night to me that usually only happens when my mother does my hair," Chelby explained.

"Wait, what thing?" Shyla asked.

"You know, my abilities thing," Chelby whispered.

"Oh, that thing. Girl, why didn't you just say my Wonder Girl thing?" Shyla whispered, smiling.

"Shyla!" Chelby grunted, bumping Shyla on her arm.

"Just messing with you," Shyla replied.

"Nothing happened though, no new ability, it was weird," Chelby admitted.

"Yeah, that is weird. Oh well, lunch is almost over. You're going to gym, right?" Shyla asked.

"Of course, we have that competition thing today, right?" Chelby questioned.

"Yup, boys vs. girls, I'm ready to kick butt," Shyla replied. Just then, the school aid signaled that lunch was over, so both girls headed to the gym.

The competition between the girls vs. the boys was a fitness competition that included speed, agility, strength, flexibility, and endurance. Both groups would be tested on these skills and used as a scoring method. Chelby and Shyla were excited and confident that the girls would win.

Once it started, it was clear that winning was on the minds of all the students participating. The boys took the strength and endurance part of the event, while the girls won the flexibility and agility portion, forcing it to come to the last event for the overall winner.

With each team exhausted, it came down to this—
a 100-meter race, a 2-mile race, and lastly, a relay race.
Shyla was usually the fastest girl in gym class, but in the
flexibility event, she hurt her hamstring.

"I don't think I can run like that, Chelby. You're
going to have to take my place," Shyla said.

"No way, I'm not even that fast, and nowhere
near as fast as you. Especially not for Mike!" Chelby
replied.

Michael Clarke was the best student-athlete in the
school. Not only was he good in all sports, but he was also
one of the strongest and by far the fastest.

"Chelby, you can do it. Come on!" Shyla insisted,
trying to instill confidence in Chelby.

"Ok, I'll try," Chelby replied reluctantly.

The first race was the 2-mile race that included
three girls and three boys. The gym teacher lined them
all up behind a line before starting. Once all the kids
lined up evenly, he said, "On your mark! Get set! GO!"

The six kids took off running. Something unusual
happened at the very beginning of the race. Chelby was in
the lead by a large margin. She kept running faster and
faster until she was ahead by more than half the other

students. Chelby was first to cross the finish line, seconds earlier than Michael.

"Woah!" The gym teacher said, looking at his stopwatch.

"Chelby, Chelby, you won!" Shyla screamed.

Michael just shook his head in disbelief as Chelby looked around in shock. There wasn't much time for Chelby to bask in the victory because the second race started right after.

In the second race, the 100 meters, much of the same thing happened. Chelby won again. All the other girls in the gym were screaming and jumping up and down with joy, with short Shyla, the loudest in the gym.

The last event was the relay, in which Chelby was the anchor, taking Shyla's place at that position. Both the boys and girls were neck and neck at the beginning. The boys started to take the lead heading into the stretch of the race. It was up to both anchors, and Chelby was off. Catching up to Michael and then flying by him, crossing the finish line with Michael, not even halfway to the finish.

The entire gym erupted with cheers for Chelby. Even some of the boys were applauding her triumph.

Shyla couldn't take the smile off her face as she approached Chelby.

"Yo, Wonder girl, what was that?!" Shyla asked among the crowd.

As soon as Shyla said those words, 'Wonder Girl', Chelby realized what happened. "I'll tell you later," Chelby said, gasping for air.

As Chelby tried to gather her breath, crouched over with her hands on her knees, the gym teacher approached her.

"Wow, Chelby, where have you been hiding all that speed," the gym teacher said in amazement.

"Uh, I don't know, guess I just got lucky," Chelby replied, shrugging her shoulders. The gym teacher put his hand on top of Chelby's back to bring her to the side to talk with her in private, separating her from the other students.

"Chelby, you know you beat Mike three times? That wasn't luck. He's the fastest in the school. You know that, right?" he said.

"Yeah, I know, but I think I just got lucky today," Chelby replied, attempting to downplay the victory.

"I don't think so, Chelby. I think you have some real talent there. Do you think you would be interested in joining the track team we have here at the school? It can lead to great opportunities," the gym teacher asked.

"I really don't think so, but I'll talk it over with my mother, and we'll see," Chelby responded.

"Ok, please let me know. You can come to the gym or my office at any time to speak with me," the gym teacher replied.

"Ok, thank you. See you later," Chelby said, walking towards Shyla.

"What did he have to talk to you about?" Shyla asked as both she and Chelby walked to the locker room to get changed.

"He asked me if I wanted to join the track team for the school. I didn't even know they had one," Chelby admitted.

"Wow, yeah, they do. So, what did you tell him?" Shyla asked.

"I told him I'd think about it, but I was just being polite. I'm not joining the team," Chelby said. "Why not?" Shyla asked.

Chelby got closer to Shyla, so she wouldn't have to speak out loud. "Cause I'm not really fast, Shyla, it's because of my abilities, my hair," Chelby whispered.

"Oh, but...," Shyla said before Chelby continued.

"Last night, I put my hair in a ponytail, then I felt the annoying pain and itching I usually get before a new ability. The only thing was that after I was ok, nothing happened, as far as any weird abilities, until now," Chelby explained.

"Oh, now I get it, makes sense, but I thought your mother had to do your hair for that to happen. Or that you had to be under the dryer or something," Shyla replied.

"I know, I did too, but guess I was wrong," Chelby responded.

"Dang, I didn't know what was going on. I was just trying to be your biggest cheerleader. That was awesome!" Shyla admitted.

"I know; I could hear you the entire race," Chelby said, laughing.

"Hey, that's what sidekicks are for," Shyla responded, winking her eye.

"You ready?" Chelby asked.

"Yeah, I been ready. I was waiting for you," Shyla replied, gathering her things off the small bench to head back to class.

After school, the girls met up in front to talk before heading home.

"You going home, Chelby?" Shyla asked.

"Um, Nah, I'm going to check my mother at the shop. Do you want to come?" Chelby asked.

"Nah, I have dance today," Shyla replied.

"Oh, that's right, but your leg," Chelby responded. "

Yeah, it's still sore, but I'm going to try and give it a go. If I can't, I'll just watch and support the other girls," Shyla responded.

"Awe, such a good teammate," Chelby mentioned, smiling.

"Whatever, punk, I'll call you later from my mother's phone, ok?" Shyla said.

"Ok, cool," Chelby replied. They hugged one another goodbye before Chelby began walking down the block towards her mother's shop.

As Chelby approached the end of the block, Shyla could see a man slowly walking towards Chelby. At first glance, she thought nothing of it, but although from a distance, the man looked familiar to her. Shyla squinted her eyes, trying to figure out why this man seemed so familiar. The man was steps away when Shyla figured out who the man was.

"Chelby, look out!" Shyla screamed down the block. Shyla's voice made Chelby turn around, facing her with the man that was behind her.

"Remember me, demon! You need to come with me now and tell the cops the truth!" The man said. It was the same man that was in Ms. Kaylie's house. The man reached to grab Chelby on the wrist, but she broke away and started to run.

The man began to chase after her, reaching out to grab her. He was directly behind Chelby when she looked back, so she turned her head back around forward in fright to focus on getting away. The next time she looked back, she was already two blocks ahead of him. "I'm gonna tell them what you are, demon!" he shouted as he gave up the chase.

Chelby stopped to catch her breath for the moment but then continued to run to her mother's shop. Once at her mother's shop, she busted through the doors frantically and headed to where her mother was, startling the customers and some of the employees.

"Chelby, what's wrong?" her mother asked. Chelby, still sweating from the run, tried to speak but was still gasping for air. Mia brought her to the back of the salon, where she could talk to Chelby privately. Mia handed her a cup of water as she rubbed Chelby's back. Finally, Chelby calmed down enough to speak.

"What happened, Chelby?" Mia asked.

"The man, Mom, the man from Ms. Kaylie's house, he's after me!" Chelby gasped.

"What? Oh my God!" Mia replied. Mia grabbed her phone and went outside to call the police as Chelby looked on through the salon's glass windows. After Mia contacted the police, she rushed back inside to Chelby.

"Just sit put and stay calm. You're safe now," Mia assured. Chelby nodded her head yes, still shaken up from the encounter with the man. As Chelby sat in the back of her mother's salon, she wondered if the abilities she now possessed were worth all the stress it was causing for her and her family.

"The police are on their way. I'm gonna go back outside to call your father now. You'll be ok, right?" Mia questioned.

"Ok, Mom. Yes, I'll be fine," Chelby replied.

Her father's words of encouragement played over and over in her head at that very moment. Chelby knew that her father was trying to instill courage and confidence in her, and with that, he hoped, she realized the abilities she was receiving were a gift from God. It sure didn't feel that way to Chelby; it felt more like a curse than a blessing to her. Only time would tell whether her feelings were correct or her father's insight. One thing was for sure; this was just the beginning of **Chelby's Hairoics.**

About the Author

    Sean Hunter was born and raised in the busy borough of Queens, New York. After being a mailman for over 12 years, ironically, he hopes to deliver inspiration to readers that come across his work. Sean values his family and faith, most notably in his life. He is a dedicated husband and father of three brilliant young children. His oldest, 9-year-old Cheyenne Hunter, inspired him to write Chelby's Hairoics. After sitting down one Sunday morning inside a college library nearby their apartment, the two brainstormed to write a book. Sean credits Cheyenne with naming every character in Chelby's Hairoics. He has aspirations of becoming a full-time writer, with hopes of reaching readers all over the world. The second installment of *Chelby's Hairoics* is already in the making. Stay tuned.

CPSIA information can be obtained
at www.ICGtesting.com
Printed in the USA
LVHW081944110222
710959LV00003B/33